The Book of Dead Days

'you're in safe hands with Sedgwick. Here is a macabre melodrama inventively told.'   Philip Ardagh, *Guardian*

'Sedgwick has created a world as dark and compelling as the story he tells.'   *Mail on Sunday*

'an impressively atmospheric novel . . . *The Book of Dead Days* is deliciously gothic in atmosphere and gripping to read.'   *Books for Keeps*

The finely-drawn characters and enthralling story-telling make this Sedgwick's greatest work to date.'
Joanne Owen, *The Bookseller*

'a compelling story, gloriously gothic, with a taut plot, an intriguing setting and a very real sense of impending evil. I particularly enjoyed the spine-tingling climactic chase, the ambiguous characters and the mixture of primitive science and dark magic. The nameless, crumbling city is vividly imagined, and provides a background rich enough to support several sequels, which I shall look forward to reading in their turn.'   Philip Reeve

'a dark and compelling novel written in a beautiful and evocative style . . . Marcus Sedgwick is one of the UK's brightest stars . . . one of the most compelling storywriters around.'   Claudia Mody, *The Bookseller*

'Sedgwick's plotting is tight and ingenious . . . a gripping read that is highly enjoyable on so many levels.'   *S F Revu*

Also by Marcus Sedgwick

The Dark Flight Down
The Dark Horse
Floodland
The Foreshadowing
Witch Hill

The Book of Dead Days

Marcus Sedgwick

A Dolphin
Paperback

For Julian and Isabel

First published in Great Britain in 2003
by Orion Children's Books
This edition published 2004 by Dolphin paperbacks
a division of the Orion Publishing Group Ltd
Orion House
5 Upper St Martin's Lane
London WC2H 9EA

10 9 8 7

A catalogue record for this book
is available from the British Library

Typeset at The Spartan Press Ltd,
Lymington, Hants

Printed in Great Britain by
Clays Ltd, St Ives plc

ISBN-10 1 84255 267 8
ISBN-13 978 1 84255 267 4

www.orionbooks.co.uk

Author's Note

Have you ever felt the stillness of that strange, quiet time between Christmas and New Year? To me these are Dead Days. Days when the doors between our own world and the unseen one that lies just beneath the surface are opened.

In this time that is no-time, the pagan power of the ancient mid-winter feast is with us. All times become one. That's how it seems to me, but I'm not the first to explore the dead days. I drew on ancient Egyptian and Aztec systems, both of which created myths to explain the addition of the five extra days needed to correct their calendars to the solar year. To the Egyptians these days were a gift from the gods; to the Aztecs, they were days of evil omen. Of course, these days bore no relation to our mid-winter, but it seemed that if days out of time belonged anywhere, it was here.

Then a world began to grow, or rather a city so huge and rambling that it is a world in itself. The City is inspired by magical places, like Paris, with its miles of unseen catacombs, Bologna, with its hidden canal system, and Krakow, with its overcrowded cemeteries and, at Christmas, lots and lots of snow.

I placed it at a time with one foot in the superstitious ancient world and one in the rational modern one, when science was starting to become the rigorous discipline it is now, but when, to the uninitiated, early experiments with electricity and magnetism must have appeared to be magic.

And when perhaps genuine magic was still to be found, especially during the Dead Days which, although they come but once a year, are with us always, just hidden from view, waiting.

I'd like to thank all the wonderful people at Orion, but especially Fiona, whose help in navigating *The Book of Dead Days* has been invaluable.

Horsham, West Sussex
31st December 2002

December 29th

The Day of the Clever Contributor

1

Darkness.

Two hours to midnight. Boy sat crouched in the box.

As usual, his legs were going to sleep under him, tucked up in the tiny dark space hidden inside the cabinet. Above him, he could hear Valerian going through his routine. Boy could only hear his voice as if from far-off, and tried to work out where he had got to. It wouldn't do to miss the cue; it wouldn't do at all. But Boy knew he didn't really need to worry. He used to try to count his way to it, but had always got lost somewhere, and anyway, there was no need – the cue was obvious enough.

Boy tried to shift his weight ever so slightly, attempting to get some feeling back in his legs. It was no good. The box had been designed specifically for him, and Valerian had seen to it that there was no more than half an inch to spare in any direction.

Suddenly there was a solid thump on the top of the box: the first cue, which meant 'Get ready, Boy.'

Boy heard a noise from the audience, faintly. He couldn't see them, but he knew what the noise meant. It was a murmur of expectation. Valerian had just stepped on to the cabinet and was even now whipping the crowd into greater excitement as he outlined the extraordinary nature of the sight they were about to see.

Boy even caught some of Valerian's words through the hefty oak panels of the cabinet.

'. . . most miraculous . . . feat of obscure . . .'

Oh-ho! thought Boy. *That means we're nearly there.*

'. . . the Man in Two Halves Illusion . . .'

He readied himself, flexing his toes inside the boots, three sizes too big for him. Thump! Thump!

The cue! Boy went to stamp his legs out through the hinged flap at the end of the box, but was suddenly hit by a powerful cramp. His toes curled painfully under him and he instantly felt sick. If he were to ruin it . . .

Desperately he tried to kick again. Still the cramp ate up his legs like a snake, biting, making him unable to move them.

Thump! Thump!

Valerian was getting cross. Boy shuddered as thoughts of what he might do to him passed through his mind. He made one last effort and shoved again. At last his legs responded and he stuck them out of the end of the box, wearing the huge boots identical to the ones Valerian was wearing.

Now, straightened out, Boy waved his legs a little. He knew this would be safe, because he was supposed to wiggle them at this point, to show they were real. They were supposed to be Valerian's, hence the matching boots.

As Valerian had got into the front half of the box, Boy's legs had not appeared where they should have done and the illusion must have been in danger. But Boy seemed to have got away with it. Now his legs were sticking through the flap, the pain began to ease a bit. He got a little more air and could hear better too.

Valerian shouted.

4

'Behold!'

Boy felt his box start to move stage left. He heard the audience begin to gasp as they understood (at last) what was happening.

'Look!' he heard someone cry. 'He's gone in half!'

It was true. From where the audience sat, they could see Valerian's head and shoulders projecting from one half of the box, while his legs moved away from him in the other part of the contraption. The single cabinet had become two boxes, running on metal tracks. There was a clear space between the two parts of his body, and the crowd went wild.

'It's true!' shouted a woman's voice, somewhere near the front, Boy thought.

Of course it was not true. It was an illusion. Although Boy knew full well what the audience were thinking as the halves of Valerian's body went in opposite directions across the stage, he knew how it was done. He was, after all, *in* on the trick. Boy felt himself smile as the crowd began to applaud wildly. Then he remembered the fiasco with his legs, and the smile faded. What would Valerian say?

Sober again, Boy prepared to pull himself back in at the right time. He could sense the automatic mechanism of the contraption begin to turn the heavy brass cogs in reverse as the two halves of the box drew back together. He felt the boxes bump gently. His cue. He felt himself panicking. He whipped his legs back inside just as Valerian stepped out of the other half of the device. Boy timed it perfectly and now, cramped back in the box, breathed as deep a breath as he could. He felt the machine being trundled off stage. It was being cleared for the finale while Valerian took the applause of the crowd.

Off-stage, Boy pushed the lid of the cabinet up with his head until there was enough space to lift it with his hands.

'Out you come, then,' said a stage hand.

Boy took his hand gratefully, his legs still not working properly. He climbed out and stood for a moment in the wings, rubbing his sore calves and watching as Valerian began his grand finale.

The Fairyland Vanishing Illusion.

Boy was not needed for this part of the act. He watched Valerian from the side of the stage.

How many times has he done this? Boy wondered. He had forgotten how long he had been working for Valerian, but it was years. Boy could only guess at how many thousand times he had hidden in boxes, pulled levers, set off thunder-flashes and opened trapdoors. He helped Valerian with trick after trick, week after week in the Great Theatre, which was as much of a home as anywhere to Boy. In recent years he had probably spent as much time in the theatre as he had in his room in Valerian's house, known as the Yellow House, back in the Old Quarter.

Boy decided to watch the grand finale from the front of the theatre, but not with the audience. He had a special place, and he wanted to be as far away as he could when Valerian came off stage.

He made his way off the stage, past the painted canvas scenery drops and ropes and wires that cluttered the world just beyond the view of the public, pushing past hands and other performers. Briefly, he glanced at Snake-girl, who sat braiding her hair in a corner, then hurried by the actors who'd finished their rowdy routine immediately before Snake-girl's act, rounded a corner and bumped straight into someone.

It was Willow, the girl who helped Madame Beauchance, a rather fat singer, into her costumes. Willow was just like her name, thin and wan. Madame had joined the theatre about a year ago, and Willow had immediately been made her servant. Boy had only spoken to Willow properly once, though. Madame had been screaming for hot water in her dressing room, and Boy had given her a freshly-boiled jug he was taking to Valerian. Afterwards he didn't know why he'd done it, and he'd got in trouble with Valerian over it, too.

'Can't you look where you're going?' Willow said, then saw who it was.

'Oh, it's you,' she added, and rushed past before Boy could say anything. Fetching something for Madame, no doubt. Her mistress was difficult, though nothing like Valerian was to him. No one was like Valerian.

'Sorry,' said Boy, but she had gone.

Boy moved on. He had other things to worry about. He knew something was going on. Something with his master. Valerian had always been erratic, sour-tempered and unpredictable. Violent.

Now he was these things. But something else as well that Boy had never seen before. He couldn't quite put it into words, but if he had really thought about it he might have realised that Valerian was preoccupied. Worried. Maybe even scared. But it would never have occurred to Boy that Valerian could be scared. It was Boy who did the being scared and the worrying – always waiting to get a hiding for any slight mistake he made.

He headed for the stairs. A group of musicians blocked the way.

'You all done for tonight, Boy?' asked the violinist, an oldish man with a bent nose.

Boy didn't answer, but forced a smile and squeezed past.

'Poor monkey,' he heard another of them say as he made his way to the secret gallery in the 'gods' above the highest row of boxes. A tiny staircase led almost up to the roof space

7

and opened on to a tiny corridor. He wasn't really allowed in the box. No one was. It was a secret that only Korp, the director of the Great Theatre, was supposed to know about, though in fact everyone did.

The door was locked, but Boy took a piece of metal from his pocket and flicked the three tumblers of the lock in no time at all. He had learned one or two things from Valerian in their time together. In fact, apart from what he'd picked up living on the streets, most of what Boy knew about anything had been taught him by Valerian.

He dropped down the couple of feet into the box. There was the little stool covered in red velvet and the small hollow table inside which Boy knew was a bottle of the director's favourite schnapps. In the front of the box was a small window. Boy carefully lifted the blind that covered the glassless hole, and peered forward. The glow from the foot-lights sparkled in his eyes.

Boy knew a lot about Valerian's tricks. He helped perform many of them and helped assemble others. But the grand finale was something very different. So spectacular was this illusion that Valerian was known throughout the whole City for it. It was probably for this trick alone that the Great Theatre was still in business.

The theatre lay in the heart of what had once been the most glamorous part of the City, the Arts Quarter, now fallen into decadence and ruin. The other acts that performed there were by and large terrible. The crowds would eat and drink and talk and laugh throughout the evening, paying little or no attention to what passed on stage. They had come for one thing. Many came night after night to see the Fairyland Vanishing Illusion. Others, new arrivals in town, travellers from distant parts maybe, were about to see it for the first time.

Boy knew nothing of the workings of this trick. He had seen it a thousand times, maybe more, and still marvelled every time. He supposed that it was too valuable, too extraordinary or too complicated for Valerian to tell anyone how it worked.

By the time Boy got up to the box, Valerian was already well into the piece. Boy craned his neck so that his nose was projecting a little through the view-hole.

The Illusion featured a short play about a drunkard who stumbles across a gathering of pixies dancing on the mountainside. They disappear back to fairyland, but the man overhears their secret words and follows them. He captures one of the little people and brings him back to the human world, determined to make his fortune with the fairy.

Valerian was reaching the climax of the show. He moved to the mouth of a cabinet built into a tree-trunk, stage right. Stage left was an identical affair. He was acting without joy or passion. He knew he didn't even have to try to inject any excitement into the audience. They were already beside themselves with anticipation.

Boy watched him carefully. Something was wrong – Valerian seemed even more uninterested than usual. He seemed impatient, in a rush to get it done with. A note had been delivered to Valerian just before the show, and Boy wondered if his strange mood had anything to do with that. He had grown sombre as he'd read.

On stage, Valerian spoke the lines as he had many times before.

'What did those little people say?' he asked, staring at the ceiling, addressing no one in particular.

'Aha! I have it!'

Valerian stepped into the tree-trunk cabinet.

'Ho! And away to fairyland!'

9

And he vanished. No more than half a second later there was a wisp of smoke from the second tree-trunk and he reappeared, holding a tiny human-like figure in his hands. The thing was tiny, cupped in his hands, and seemed, at least, to be alive. It wriggled in his hands and you would swear you could hear a little voice coming from it. It appeared to be dressed in leaves and flowers. It could have been male or female, but it was certainly a fairy.

Then, just as Valerian, playing the drunkard, appeared to have achieved his goal, there was a double flash of lightning, the fairy seemed to grow for a split second to the size of a man, and then both it and Valerian vanished again, back to fairyland.

The crowd, knowing this to be the pinnacle of the performance, erupted into huge cheers and shouts of delight.

Boy sat back on the red velvet stool and felt something dig into his back. He looked round and jumped out of his skin. Valerian sat behind him, glowering.

'You, Boy,' he said, 'have let me down.'

2

'Name the five principles of Cavallo,' Valerian snapped.

They hurried through the dark streets of the City – the vast, ancient City that sprawled away into the darkness around them in all its rotting magnificence, a tangled mess of grand streets and vulgar alleys, spent and decrepit. Fat houses squatted on either side of them like wild animals lurking in the gloom.

The City. Once it had been the capital of a powerful empire, which now only existed in the peculiar mind of Frederick, the octogenarian Emperor, shut away somewhere behind the high walls of the Palace.

The Emperor's warped memories were utterly unknown to Boy. *His* world began and ended with Valerian. As the two of them made their way along a particularly horrid street called Cat's End, the midnight bells began to strike. The 27th of December had begun.

Valerian strode a pace ahead of Boy, but held his coat tails to pull Boy half-running, half stumbling along behind. He was testing Boy in mind as well as body.

'Well?' he barked.

'Mystery,' Boy panted as they sped along. 'Mystery and preparation and . . . sorry.'

He stumbled on a cobblestone. Valerian dragged him

practically in the air around a corner and into a side street. A short-cut home.

'What?' yelled Valerian. 'Mystery and preparation and *what*?'

'Direction?'

'*Mis*-direction, you goat!'

'Mis-direction,' said Boy, and then before Valerian had a chance to shout again, 'and practice and skill. Natural skill,' he added hurriedly.

Valerian grunted in satisfaction, but didn't slow the pace. Boy stumbled after him, having trouble moving his legs properly as he was pulled sideways by the tails of his coat.

After the show, Valerian had glared at Boy for a good long while, so there was no doubt that Boy was in a great deal of trouble. Then he had dragged him out of the box, along the tiny passageway, down the stairs and out into the night without even bothering to collect the money for the performance. Boy had hardly had time to think, but there was something bothering him badly. It had taken him at least three minutes to get from the side of the stage to the box. It had taken Valerian no more than a couple of seconds. At least that was how it seemed, but Boy knew from experience not to trust anything he saw Valerian do. You could never be sure, not really.

They moved on through the City, Valerian clutching Boy's coat tails, looking, from a distance, like some strange beast. They were in Gutter Street. Although there were no street signs in this part of the City (it was much too down-at-heel for refinements like that), nevertheless Boy knew where he was. They passed the Green Bird Inn. Boy had been hoping they might stop for Valerian to have a drink or two. Or more. Then he might have forgotten about Boy's slip-up.

12

But he strode by without even a glance at the tavern. Boy gulped and staggered on.

'All right then,' said Valerian. 'And if you don't observe the Five Principles you may as well just rely on luck, which is what you made us do tonight. Anyone half sober or with half a mind would have seen–'

'I'm sorry,' said Boy.

Valerian stopped suddenly and Boy ran into the back of him. He looked down into Boy's eyes.

'Well,' he said, and his voice was suddenly quiet, 'well, it's not important. Really.'

He dropped Boy's coat tails and began to head for home, still walking fast.

Boy had been thrashed by Valerian before for much less than this. More confused than ever, he watched him go for a moment. Valerian's tall figure, his longish greying hair flowing behind him, was about to disappear round another corner. Although Boy knew the area, he grew alarmed.

Unpleasant things had been happening in the City recently. Even in the better areas, horror was not unknown. There had been a spate of murders, and the inns, taverns, salons and courts had been full of talk of these crimes. The murders were remarkable for their particularly gory nature, with the bodies sometimes drained of blood. Rumours had spread of the ghastly apparition responsible – 'The Phantom'. There had also been a series of grave-robbings in some of the many cemeteries around the huge City. Many people thought the two were linked.

'Hey!' Boy cried. 'Wait for me!'

It was deep into the night, and they were now in one of the worst parts of the City. Nearly home.

3

Korp, the director of the theatre, began closing up. Half an hour ago he had finally managed to throw the last drunken idiot out, and before he'd even hit the mud of the alley had slammed the door after him. He didn't have to worry about being too nice to his customers. They would come night after night, as long as Valerian kept doing that thing about fairies.

Director Korp sat for a while in his office, staring into space. He felt old and tired and fat, because he was. He daydreamed, remembering days when he had travelled the continent with the greatest show ever assembled. The show had included a giant, five midgets, a two-headed calf, a snake-woman, a disappearing lady, a levitating man, twin wild boys, and many, many more. It was all far behind him, and though he missed the excitement of his youth, he had a theatre to run now, and he would run it as best he could till the day he died.

On the walls around him hung portraits of some of the stars who had appeared in his theatre. There were paintings of Cavallo the Great, a legendary magician. There was Grolsch, a famous escapologist whose career had come to an untimely end one night when he had failed to escape, and Bertrand Black, a bear-tamer who had had a similarly rapid demise on stage. But all the faces were from days long gone, when things had been different, more lucrative.

Korp scratched his bald head for a minute or so, then without looking down, put his hand into a drawer in the ornate desk at which he was sitting. He fumbled around, still without looking. He put his hand on his pistol, and shoved it aside. It wasn't what he wanted.

'Yeush!' he said, with a frown. 'Where's it gone?'

Then he remembered the bottle he'd left in his 'secret' box. Wearily he got to his feet and made his way down the darkened corridors back-stage. As he passed one of the dressing rooms he noticed a light.

'Who's there?' he called.

'Oh, Director,' said a voice from inside. 'It is Madame.'

He stuck his head around the door.

'Ah!' he said. 'Madame! Madame Beauchance! May I say how exquisitely you sang tonight!' He smiled a wide smile.

Madame Beauchance appeared to ignore this compliment.

'It will have to change,' she said.

'Madame?'

Now Korp noticed the girl, Beauchance's assistant, kneeling at the singer's feet and rubbing her ankles. The girl glanced up at him.

'Madame means . . . ?' he began again.

'I mean', said Madame, not even looking at Korp, 'that I will not continue to appear in an *inferior* position. To that prestidigitator.'

Korp blinked.

He felt tired. He wanted to be in bed with Lily curled up around his feet. Lily was his dog.

'The magician,' whispered the girl, almost unheard.

'Exactly!' cried Madame Beauchance.
'Ah!' said Korp. 'Oh!'
Valerian.

4

Midnight.

Boy had caught up with Valerian at the top of the next alley – a little gutter of a lane called Blind Man's Stick, where the roof-tiles of the buildings either side were close enough to touch in places. Here and there it was possible to catch a glimpse of the night sky between them, but Boy was not interested in the stars. Not yet.

He clung tightly to Valerian as they made their way quickly along the foul-smelling culvert. A minute later they emerged into a relatively wide street. An open drain ran down its middle. Valerian stepped across it in a single stride. Boy, small for his years, leapt the gap, slipping as he landed.

He sat dazed in the stream then, realising where he was, leapt to his feet.

'Oh!' he said. 'Ugh!'

Boy looked himself up and down. His bottom half was covered in unnameable filth.

'Ugh! Oh!'

Valerian did not even glance back.

Boy limped after him. They turned a corner and crossed a final street.

Valerian stopped for a moment at a wrought iron gate let

17

into a high stone wall. He rattled one of the big keys from his pocket in the lock, and shoved the gate open. Only now did he look back long enough to be sure Boy had got through the gate with him, then swung it shut and rattled its lock one more time.

They were home.

Boy stood dripping, trying not to smell himself as he waited in the small walled courtyard that lay between the iron gate and the front door.

Valerian opened the door with another key from the huge bunch and went inside.

The house seemed to tense as Valerian shut the door behind them both. He said nothing but stood absolutely still, as if waiting. Then he turned and looked at Boy.

'What is that vile stench?' he barked.

Boy shrugged.

'I fell over . . .'

'For God's sake go and get clean! Then come to the tower.'

'Yes, sir,' said Boy.

He shuffled down one of the corridors that led off the hall.

'And be quick. You have work to do!'

5

Boy ran along two corridors and then up three flights of
rickety wooden stairs to his room. 'Room' was perhaps something of an exaggeration. Room, or space, was one thing the
place he slept in did not have. There was a mattress, which
was actually quite comfortable though it was a shame,
thought Boy, that he did not get to spend more time on it.
The smallest of openings ('window' would have been too
grand a word for it) let in some light. This was in the sloping
roof that made up one wall of his room. His bed lay against
the single vertical wall, the entrance lurked in one of the
triangular ends to the space, and in the opposite one was a
tiny door behind which was an even tinier cupboard. Inside
the cupboard were all Boy's possessions. A spoon he'd found
in the street and particularly liked. A pair of old boots that
were too small and worn out to wear any more. A silk scarf
he'd stolen from a rich lady, but which was too nice to wear.
Some small empty tins that nested inside each other and
some pencils which Valerian had given him to practise his
writing.

This was his room.

The day Valerian had put him in it, Boy had come straight
back down and eventually found Valerian sipping port in the
library.

'But I can't stand up in it,' Boy had complained.

'Then kneel down, Boy,' Valerian had said, and cuffed him round the ear.

Boy was used to clambering about in small spaces. He seemed to spend his life doing it: on stage in coffin-like cabinets and off-stage in the theatre too, slithering along to Korp's supposedly secret box. At home, the last part of his journey meant climbing up a small ladder from the third-floor landing and hunching up to travel down a tiny, low-ceilinged corridor tucked into the roof space that led to his room.

Small, cramped, dark spaces had filled Boy's life. He had even been hiding in one the day he was found by Valerian in an old church, St Colette's. Boy had crammed his narrow frame into a space at the top of a pillar in the nave. It was a long time ago – he had little idea when. Since he had been working for Valerian he had not seen much daylight, never mind been allowed access to such private information as what time it was, or what day or month, for that matter. It was, in fact, March the 6th when Valerian had found Boy, but Boy didn't know that. Only Valerian knew about dates and times, places and names and the like. Boy worked for him, and that was the end of the story. When he wasn't working Boy would climb up to his room and collapse on the tiny mattress, exhausted.

And the beginning of the story, when Valerian had found Boy? He had been in a tiny dark hole then, too. That was probably why Valerian had chosen him, taken him on – because of his expertise in squeezing into ridiculously small spaces. Boy had forgotten much of the detail now; it was long long ago, and unimportant compared to the business of every day. Every day, trying to avoid trouble, trying to avoid upsetting him or getting something wrong and . . .

He could remember one thing about it all though. From the stupidly small gap made where the arch fluted away from the pillar, he had seen Valerian for the first time. He was deep in discussion with someone Boy now knew to be Korp, from the theatre.

Even then Valerian looked haggard and pale. His nose, long and fine, twitched in the dusty atmosphere of the old church. His skin was grey, so was his hair. He looked like a dead man walking. His blue eyes, however, were full of life, and his gaze roamed the dark spaces around him.

Then Boy had heard his midnight rumble of a voice, so deep the stone he was clinging to shivered with it.

'The doctor,' intoned Valerian, 'pronounced me either dangerously sick or dead.'

It was while trying to understand the strangeness of those words that Boy had lost his grip and plummeted to the flag floor of the church, where he lay looking up at Valerian, scratching his nose nervously, his short, cropped black hair stuck up at interesting angles the way it always did.

'O-ho!' Valerian had said. 'What have we here?'

And so they had met.

Boy pulled off his reeking clothes and stood naked in his dark space. He wondered what to do. The pile of clothes at his feet stank up at him. There was no water in his room. The only room with a bath was on the first floor. He had no other clothes, just a long winter overcoat. But if he put that on now he would get it covered in the same filth that was still slimed over his legs.

He sighed, picked up the pile of dirty clothes and the coat and crept back along the tube to the ladder.

He dropped the clothes down to the third-floor landing, and followed them, shivering as he went.

6

Boy sat, scratching his nose. He was nervous because
Valerian was pacing up and down the Tower room, criss-
crossing the floor a dozen times, then pausing, staring into
space for a short while before resuming his compulsive
journey from the tall, narrow window in one of the sloping
walls to the top of the spiral staircase, which was the only
means of access by foot to the Tower. Large or heavy items
had to be winched into the Tower through a trapdoor in the
floor. Despite his nerves Boy noticed that, as usual, Valerian
was perfectly happy to stride over the trapdoor. Boy knew
the hatch was strong enough, but he would never walk over
it, just in case. The trapdoor opened above the landing on
the second floor; it was quite a drop.

The rest of the Tower room was filled with clutter, paraphernalia, ephemera, equipment, things and mechanisms
of all descriptions. Astrolabes, hourglasses, armillary spheres,
sextants, alembics, retorts, reduction dishes, mortars with
pestles, crystals, locks with and without keys, knives, dag-
gers, wands of brass and wands of wood, pots, bottles and jars
were just some of the odds and ends that lay scattered
around the Tower.

Boy knew what some of them were – things they used on
stage. As for those he didn't understand, Boy often won-

dered what they might be. Maybe they were more, and as yet untried, pieces of magical equipment for the act, though Boy had his doubts.

There was the great leather armchair in which Valerian would sit, often in pensive mood, brooding over Boy knew not what, and there were books. Piles and piles and piles of books of all shapes and sizes, leaning at precarious angles against walls and chairs, and, Boy assumed, about all sorts of things.

Right in the middle of the Tower stood the machine. Boy always had trouble remembering what it was called. As he sat, waiting for Valerian to say or do something, he tried to remember its name. It had been designed and built by a man called Kepler, who was the closest thing Valerian had to a friend.

Boy had never seen the machine working, but since it had been installed Valerian had spent even more time in the Tower. It had a strange Latin name, and now Boy remembered that it translated as 'dark room'.

'Do you have no grasp of Latin at all?' Valerian had barked at him. Boy had shaken his head.

Valerian had cursed.

'Idiot boy! If you knew some Latin you would know what it meant! Dark. Room. Camera – room. Obscura – dark. See?'

Boy had smiled nervously, pretending he understood.

'Oh, why do I try to teach you anything!' Valerian had snapped, and sat back in his leather armchair.

'Camera obscura' – that was it!

Now Boy had remembered he felt pleased with himself, and sat, wondering what on earth it was that the thing did.

Valerian kept on walking. Boy sat in just his overcoat, scratching his nose harder.

Then Valerian stopped.

'Boy,' he said, 'I have a job for you.'

I was afraid you'd say that, thought Boy.

'Yes,' said Boy. 'Whatever I can do–'

'You can be quiet!' Valerian snapped. 'Just listen, then do. All right?'

Oh, fine, thought Boy.

He didn't say anything, but nodded.

'I . . .' Valerian began, not looking at Boy but out of the window and across the nightscape of the City. 'We . . . I . . . have a problem. Things are not what they were. Things . . .' he continued, 'are . . . different now. Different. They have changed.'

He stopped and looked at Boy.

'Clear?' he said.

Boy nodded furiously.

'Things have not happened as I had intended and now – and now time is not on our side. Far from it. We must act.'

Boy nodded some more.

'Things have not gone . . . according to plan. So I have a job for you. Tonight.'

'Tonight?' asked Boy, then shut his mouth quickly.

'Yes. Tonight. The Trumpet. You know it?'

Boy grimaced. The Trumpet was an inn about three miles away, near the river-docks. He had been there before, and on leaving had prayed that would be his first and last visit.

'You must go and get something for me. Some information. Tonight. Good. Then go. Look for an ugly man. His name's Green.'

Boy nodded.

'Say I sent you and tell him to give you the information. Then come back here. Do nothing else. Talk to no one else.'

Boy hesitated. He wondered whether he dared risk a question.

May as well, he thought.

'Valerian,' he said carefully, 'what is the information? How will I know what he tells me is right?'

'You won't!' snapped Valerian. 'Just go! And do not get it wrong!'

Boy nodded at him.

'And be quick,' said Valerian coldly.

Boy waited, questions playing across his face.

'So what are you waiting for?' Valerian yelled.

Boy jumped to his feet and fled down the stairs.

7

By the time Korp got the fat singer out of his theatre, and the girl too, it was late. There was no way he could move Valerian down the running order, but he had been pleased enough to get Madame from her previous permanent engagement in a foreign city, many, many miles away. He sighed as he made his way up to his little loft. This was no mean feat due to his considerable proportions and the narrowness of the passage.

He made it to the door, and noticed immediately that it was not locked. Not only that, but the little door swung open on its concealed hinges.

He cursed everyone in the Company, then collapsed into the box. Flicking the lid of the table with one foot, he sank his teeth into the cork of the bottle, removed it and then he drank, long and deep.

He sighed.

Suddenly he heard a noise. It sounded like footsteps, coming from the stage. He leant forward, peering out through the view-hole.

Nothing. At least, it was too dark to see anything. He held his breath.

Still nothing. Just as he had decided he was imagining it, he heard the sound again.

He peered down into the gloom of the auditorium.

His eyes grew wide in their sockets.

8

Boy wasted half an hour while he wondered whether to risk asking Valerian what he should do about the fact that he had no dry clothes. Then, deciding it was best not to bother him, Boy had set out for the Trumpet dressed in his winter overcoat, with a piece of sacking for leggings, and his boots, which he had wiped as clean as he could.

He left, slamming the door behind him. Boy was allowed no keys to the house, but Valerian had designed a special lock that operated automatically when the door was pulled shut. You needed no key to lock the door, just one to open it again. And this was not a lock that Boy could unpick. He knew because he had tried. Shortly after Valerian had shown him how to pick simple locks with a twist of metal, Boy had found himself locked out.

He had gone sneaking out one evening after the show, searching for an extra bite to eat. Food was never plentiful in the house – it didn't interest Valerian greatly and Boy was always trying to find more. Sometimes he could persuade one of the musicians from the theatre to buy him a meal. This particular evening he'd dined thanks to the kindness of the old violinist. Hunger having driven him to the rendez-vous, it was only upon his return that he realised he would not be able to get back into the house.

Aha! Boy said to himself. *Let's see if I've got this right.*

He hunted round in his pockets for his lock-picking metal. It had once served as the artificial tendon in a metal hand that Valerian had dismantled. When he had grown bored with it, Boy had found it just right for the job of lock-picking.

He leant closer to the lock. It was almost completely dark in the street and he peered hard at the hole. He reached forward with his makeshift key, but no sooner had he touched the metal innards of the lock with the metal tendon than he was thrown backwards across the street, landing in a heap in the gutter. His hand, in fact his whole arm, felt as though it had been bitten by a dragon.

Boy rubbed his bad arm with his other hand, cursing his luck.

Some magic device, no doubt, put by Valerian on the door to keep thieves away.

He had been in deep trouble when Valerian had found him the following morning, huddled on the doorstep, having spent a wretched freezing night outside.

Inventing was just one of Valerian's many areas of knowledge. Years ago, when more involved in the life of the Great Theatre, he had invented a system of footlights for the stage – another reason why Korp was deeply indebted to him. The lights worked on some system of chemical fire that only Valerian understood and that only he could control. They gave off a faint, yet pungent smell, but were another reason why Korp's theatre had a reputation as the best in the City.

Boy had learnt much from him because Valerian was, for all his faults, a remarkable man. But despite their years together, Boy actually knew very little about him. He would try and fit bits and pieces together, and over the years had

30

picked up enough scraps of information to put together some of his life story.

Boy knew Valerian had attended the Academy, where Kepler, the man who had recently made the camera obscura, was one of his fellow students. He knew that Valerian had studied Natural Philosophy. He had been considered a more than able scholar, with the potential to become a great one. Something had happened, Boy did not know what, but it was enough to make him fall from grace. Boy once heard Valerian say something that implied it was because of particular studies he was making. Boy gathered that he had been conducting peculiar experiments, explorations into secret or forgotten learning. Boy never found out exactly what, but it was enough to know it was something dark and forbidden.

Around this time Boy knew that Kepler and Valerian had fallen out, or at least lost touch. They had not seen each other until only a few years back. In fact, Boy could remember when Valerian started visiting Kepler in his tall and narrow house across the City, and after a while Boy would occasionally go too.

Boy also knew that Valerian had once been very wealthy, which was when he had bought the house – a huge and rambling edifice that was now a decayed shadow of its former self. It had been purchased from the family of a judge who had died. It was still an opulent building then, a worthy residence for one of the City's highest officials. But Valerian seemed to be rich no more, and over the years the house had gone to seed and the neighbourhood around it had too.

Boy did not know how he had lost his money, but Valerian was no longer rich and seemed not to care very much for anything, except the hours he spent shut away in

31

the Tower, doing heaven knows what with his infernal contraptions and reading books from the teetering piles that lay around the room.

Boy loved the house despite the large number of empty rooms and shamefully dirty corridors, if only because it was the only place he had ever called home. If he kept out of Valerian's way, or at least did nothing to upset him, Boy found a little peace inside its walls. And there was the small paved garden outside the kitchen door, where on hot days Boy would cool himself among ferns and vines that sprouted from the high, damp stone walls, making the garden a secret space. There was a small well in the centre of the paving, from which sometimes Boy fancied that he could hear rushing water, like a river far beneath him, though he knew it was just his fancy. The river was a sluggish, smelly beast, miles away from the house, and the well seemed to be just a dry, bottomless hole.

Boy put his hand against the flat panels of the door, willing it to open, but he would have to go on now. It was a cold night and he was naked under his coat except for the sack-cloth leggings. Boy hoped Valerian would still be awake when he got back, but there was every chance of that. He kept strange hours – working through the night, sometimes resting fitfully during the day and then getting up in the early evening to perform at the theatre. Boy glanced up at the Tower high above the street, but he saw no light coming from within. This was odd. It would be unlike Valerian to sleep at night! For a moment, Boy wondered if Valerian had gone out again himself. The house was so large that from his room he would not have heard the front door close.

There was nothing he could do about it now. The lock had dropped firmly behind him and he was out in the City, alone.

It was about one in the morning and the Quarter was reaching its peak of activity. It only truly seemed to come alive late at night, with street traders still about and the taverns heaving with beer and laughter. People worked long hours and for some of them this was their only chance to pretend they had a life that was something other than total drudgery.

Boy tried, as a rule, to make himself unseen, and most of the time did a good job of avoiding trouble in this way. He was neither short nor tall, but he was very thin, and by emptying his mind and avoiding people's eyes with his own, he made a fair stab at invisibility as he passed through the City at night.

The City was looking its best. Some of its unpleasantness was obscured during the festivities and holidays. As was the custom, evergreen branches had been used to decorate houses, shops and other buildings. It was also traditional to burn candles at this time, and windows everywhere twinkled with pretty lights which, once lit in the evening, burnt long into the night.

Night. It was all he seemed to see, especially during these winter days. Valerian kept Boy busy with this and that all through the small hours, until finally, just as dawn was creeping over the City, he would let him stagger off to his cot to slumber the day away. Then, shouting through all the floors of the house, Valerian would rouse Boy for another evening's performance in the theatre.

'I am a vampire,' Boy said grimly as he stole down Dead Duck Lane. 'That's it. He's a stinking vampire and now I am too!'

Realising he was talking aloud, he looked rapidly around him, but he had gone unnoticed.

Boy thought again about what had happened to Valerian.

It was only a recent thing, maybe just a few weeks or months ago. Valerian had definitely become more irritable than usual. His moods had always swung rapidly from one extreme to another, but now they seemed firmly fixed in one extreme. Surly and preoccupied, he was less violent, less vitriolic. He spent hours on end in the Tower, only emerging to get Boy to run an errand. Boy had delivered a lot of letters for him recently, and collected many in reply.

Letters, thought Boy. *Letters?*

It reminded him – there was one evening, one evening in particular, when he had delivered a letter to Kepler. Kepler lived a good way across the City, in the University Quarter.

Boy didn't like Kepler much. He wasn't sure why exactly. Maybe it was because Valerian listened intently to what Kepler had to say, but showed little or no interest in any opinions Boy might have. There was something about him Boy just didn't warm to.

Kepler was thin like Valerian, but shorter and with none of Valerian's strength. He was always muttering to himself, and tended to scurry about like a rat, Boy thought. But if it was true that Boy didn't like Kepler, it was also true that he was fascinated by him, for he was as much of a hoarder of strange devices and peculiar mechanisms as Valerian.

As well as being a Doctor of Medicine of the Human Animal, Kepler made specialised studies into the field of The Heavens. He had all sorts of equipment with which he looked up at the stars. He recorded his observations in huge leather-bound books, having noted the motions of planets, stars and moons through his metal and glass devices. Kepler had told Boy that he could then make all sorts of predictions about people and their behaviour, just by knowing when they had been born. Increasingly Boy had gone with

Valerian on his visits to Kepler's house. He would sit quietly in the corner of Kepler's room and marvel at the astounding discussions they would hold, hearing a lot, and learning a little.

Boy wished someone could tell him about *his* life, predict what would happen to *him*, just by setting his date of birth against the position of the stars. He knew, though, that even Kepler could not do that, because Boy did not know when he had been born.

Once Boy had been worried about this. He had even been bold enough to speak to Valerian about it.

'Who do you think my parents were?' he had asked. 'How could I find out?'

But Valerian had only scoffed at him.

'You will never know, nor does it matter one jot. Nor', he added, 'do you need to know. You are Boy, *my* Boy, and that is enough.'

Boy always tried to do what Valerian told him to – things were safer that way. So Boy tried not to think about the matter any more, but it was not always easy.

On this particular evening, however, when Boy had delivered the letter to Kepler, the Doctor had asked him to wait. Kepler had written a reply to Valerian. Boy had watched him as he scratched away with a sophisticated silver-nibbed fountain pen on a sheet of paper, pausing momentarily to consider his words. Kepler had sprinkled the letter with sand, then folded up the paper and started to melt some sealing wax. As he dripped blood-red wax on to the letter, and pressed his ring into it, he spoke to Boy.

'Take this to him,' he said, without looking up from what he was doing, 'and may God protect his own.'

There was something odd in his manner which Boy remembered. It was when he had taken the letter back that

Valerian's mood had really sunk. That was when it had really started.

At about two o'clock Boy stopped at the top of Pigeon Pie Alley. At the far end of the street stood The Trumpet. All hell was breaking loose inside.

Oh, just perfect! thought Boy.

9

Korp stared at the stage, watching the ghost.

At first he thought it must be the Dark Duke. An old theatre legend told how the ghost of the Dark Duke would stalk across the stage as a portent of disaster. History related how, years ago, the theatre had relied on the Duke for financial backing. If he didn't like the work the theatre was producing, he would storm across the stage during rehearsal, sometimes even during a performance. One day he had tried to stop a rehearsal and was stabbed by the lead actor, a touchy man at the best of times, whose brother had written the play in question. Since then the Dark Duke appeared at times of impending crisis, though he had not been seen in many, many years.

The theatre was in trouble. Korp had seen so many strange things in his life that he was superstitious enough to believe that. There could be no mistake about it. The only question was when.

In fact Korp was mistaken. He had only been watching the ghost for a few moments when it disappeared, leaving behind a slight cloud of dust that hung in the air, glowing.

A second later, Korp heard something behind him.

The thing slashed at Korp's body, and he fell forward, one arm and his head across the edge of the box, dying.

Boy hovered in the street, trying to decide what to do. He knew he didn't really have any choice. If Valerian wanted him to go into The Trumpet and meet a big, ugly man called Green, then he would have to do it. It was just that he didn't want to.

There was obviously a fight going on inside – Boy could tell that from where he stood, at the end of Pigeon Pie Alley. He waited, hoping things would settle down, but after a little while he changed his mind. Perhaps everyone would be too busy in the tavern to notice him; he could slip in and take a look around without being seen. Besides, he was freezing in his makeshift clothes. At least inside he'd be warm for a while, and get away from the smell of the river just a street or two away.

As he approached The Trumpet the sound of tables breaking and bottles being smashed grew louder. The inn was really rough. There was no longer a sign with its name outside – its reputation spoke for it. There was grimy glass in some of the windows, though not all by any means. The way in to The Trumpet was in a claustrophobic alley that lay in the gloom between the buildings. Boy glanced in through a window as he headed down the alley. Things were getting lively, to say the least. He took one last gulp of the foul river air, and went inside.

The noise immediately seemed ten times louder, and if the stink was bad in the street, it was worse still inside. The whole place was a lurid riot of colour, sound and smell compared to the darkness of the City's winter streets outside. The effect was overwhelming and for a minute Boy thought he might be sick. His head swam with the confusion of it all. He looked for a place to lurk.

Surprisingly, considering the noise they were making, the fight seemed only to be between two men. The bulk of the din came from the people watching, who were cheering, shouting and fighting amongst themselves.

Boy picked his way to a small table half-hidden in the space under the staircase that led upstairs.

'Beer, love?'

He looked up to see a barmaid staring at him expectantly. She held a tray of empty beer jugs in one hand and was piling short, stubby glasses up with the other.

'Well?'

Damn! thought Boy. *Money. I didn't think of that. Neither did Valerian, but that won't stop me getting a thrashing if I get this wrong.*

'I don't have any money,' he said, looking up sadly at the barmaid.

She scowled briefly, then her face softened and she smiled.

'Did you know you've got nothing on under there?' she asked, smirking.

Boy looked down and hurriedly pulled his coat shut over his legs. He thought for a moment.

'It's cold outside,' he ventured, trying to sound as miserable as he could. 'You know, on the streets . . .'

'All right,' she said, 'but just half an hour, mind, then out you go. Here, take this.'

She put one of the glasses she had collected back down in front of him, and then emptied the dregs of five beer jugs into it. She nodded at the glass now containing a couple of fingers of beer slops and smiled again.

'Better make it last, Gorgeous,' she said, and went off collecting more glasses while they were still unbroken.

Boy took one look at the beer and pushed it away.

The fight was just about over. The victor, a giant of a man, sat on the chest of the vanquished, a fat brute, raining a few last punches down on his face for good measure. But it was all for show now. Finally someone came to pull him off the fat man.

'That's enough, now. Well done.'

The giant got up and for the first time Boy saw his face. He was as ugly as a dead cat.

He seemed not to appreciate being pulled off the fat man, because he swung a fist at his would-be helper and sent him sprawling across a table.

Everyone cheered except Boy, who had a sinking feeling in his stomach. He pulled the sleeve of a toothless old man with a stick who was sitting nearby.

'Who's that?' Boy asked, but he knew the answer already.

'Eh?' said the man. 'Don't you know Jacob Green, The Green Giant?'

The man laughed, spat on the floor and waved his stick in the air for a drink.

Meanwhile Green swaggered around, taking drinks from all and sundry and downing them in a single draught. Boy looked at the giant, ugly, violent man.

Green.

The man he'd come to meet.

Boy looked at his beer.

Green sat talking loudly now to a group in a corner, playing with something tiny in his giant hands, like a child with a toy. It was a small wooden box. He was spinning it between thumb and forefinger. Then he stopped and wound a little handle coming from its side. A small tinkle of musical notes floated through the hubbub of the tavern. A music box.

Around him, two serving girls picked up bits of shattered bottles and broken chairs. It crossed Boy's mind that he did not have a clue what was going on. This was a feeling he often had working for Valerian, but things were definitely getting more peculiar. The business in Korp's box, when Valerian had materialised behind him no more than a few seconds after he'd left the stage, had unnerved him. But Boy had barely had time to puzzle over that before he'd been bundled out in the street to meet Green. Boy wondered what on earth Valerian could need from him. There was only one way to find out.

Boy looked at his beer. Picking up the glass he swigged the cloudy brown liquid straight down, wiped his mouth and took a deep breath. He stood up and made his way across the room.

11

Boy was not the only servant abroad at that moment. Back in the Quarter of the Arts, Willow ventured out into the cold night, moaning to herself, wrapping her shawl around shoulders and over her head. Her mouse-brown hair was thick and long, keeping her warm. She had been working for Madame Beauchance for a year now, ever since she had come to the Great Theatre. It was a year too long in her opinion.

The woman was large and unattractive, she was vain and arrogant, she was lazy and spiteful, and miserly too. There was, though, one thing which redeemed her, and that was her voice. It was the voice of nothing less than an angel. It was a voice that could murmur soft and low and soothe a bawling child, that could rise shrill and clear and shatter a mirror and that could slide so sweetly over a melody that a killer might sit down and weep. With her voice she had made a good career, and a small fortune that she kept to herself.

Willow had ended up working for her by chance. She had been employed as tail-carrier in her previous job, working for the Fellowship of Master Liverymen. Willow didn't know what the Fellowship actually did, but she knew what she was supposed to do, and that was enough. And besides, anything was better than life in the orphanage. The Livery-men wore fancy clothes on official occasions, including long-tailed coats. It was her job to follow behind her master, carrying the tails of his coat so they did not trail in the dirt. There were eleven other girls and boys employed likewise, one for each of the Fellowship. That was the full extent of their duties, but since there were at least two official occasions every day, they were kept busy enough carrying coat tails and brushing off mud where necessary. After three years, she had been told to take a coat to the Great Theatre where they required the costume of a Liveryman.

Willow had immediately fallen for the excitement of the place. It was thrilling. She had begged Korp for a job and had begun scrubbing floors that afternoon. She never went back to the Liverymen and they did not come looking for her – there were plenty more urchins to be had. After a week of odd jobs, Madame B had arrived and immediately demand-ed a personal assistant. Her last one, a man with a weak heart, had collapsed carrying her cases of costumes on the journey to the City.

Willow was not fond of her mistress, especially this even-ing, when she'd blamed Willow for not bringing her hair-brush. She had told Willow to go back to the theatre and get Korp to open up. None of the other hundreds of brushes she had at her lodgings was good enough, apparently, so Willow had set off back to the theatre.

That was how she found the side door to the theatre flap-ping open in the chilly night air, and how she walked cauti-ously into the auditorium, already sensing something was wrong, and how she stood halfway back in the stalls, looking at the stage, when she felt it raining on her head.

She noticed that the footlights were faintly glowing. That

too was odd – they were very expensive to run. Then she remembered she was inside and that it couldn't be raining.

She put her hand to her hair and felt the wetness. It was warm. From the dim light coming from the stage she looked at her hand and screamed.

It was covered in blood.

She looked up to see the head and shoulders of Korp's corpse sticking out of the box's window.

She screamed again.

12

Green gave Boy's throat another gentle squeeze. He had one of his huge spade-like fists wrapped around it, though not tightly.

Not yet, thought Boy.

Despite the fact that they were still in the front room of The Trumpet, and in full view of everyone in the tavern, Boy had no doubt that Green would snap his neck like a dry reed if he wanted to. This was not the sort of place where the men of the City Watch ever came. It had its own laws, and one murder or another was probably neither here nor there to these people.

Boy stood in front of Green, who sat with one arm outstretched, his fingers raising Boy on to his tiptoes. Even like this, Green was taller than him. Boy was quite glad because it meant he was not looking straight at Green's foul face. He had a wide nose, with nostrils that had obviously been split at some point or other in his colourful past. The whites of his eyes were yellow and watery, his lips were like two slugs sitting on each other. His hair was thinning and his scalp was diseased. Boy tried not to look, and anyway, he had other things to concentrate on. He had been standing precariously on tiptoe ever since he had had the nerve to approach the giant.

'What do you want?' Green had bawled.

'I . . . I . . .' stammered Boy.

'*What?*' Green yelled.

'I've been sent to–'

'Ah!' said Green. '*He* sent you, did he? Too scared to come himself! Perhaps I should just give you what I was going to give him!'

Boy nodded, and next thing he knew he was balancing on the ends of his toes.

'He sent you?'

'U-hurrrr,' squeaked Boy.

'What?' shouted Green, letting Boy drop a little on to his feet.

'Mmm.'

Green scowled, then grabbed Boy tightly again, and picking him off his feet, shook him briskly. He put him down again.

'So I see,' scoffed Green. 'Well, tell him to come himself. I only deal with him.'

'I have to find out–' began Boy, but Green grabbed him by the throat and began to squeeze. 'Tell him he's to come himself. Now get lost!'

He dropped Boy, who fell to his knees choking. Hearing the tinny notes of the music box again he looked up. Green was spinning the handle, laughing to himself, captivated by the simple tune.

Boy caught only a glimpse of it before it was hidden in Green's massive hand, but it was strange and beautiful.

Boy sat in the dirt of the floor, rubbing his sore neck.

Green lurched to his feet and sloped away from Boy across the room, pushing past people as he went.

'I need a leak!' he announced as he staggered through a door in the back.

Boy picked himself up, wondering what to do.

He waited for a few moments, then a few more, and then followed Green to the door that led outside to the latrine.

What followed next was too fast for Boy to see.

As he stepped through the door there was a flash of light and a noise like a cork popping. Then everywhere was shrouded in purple smoke.

He heard a thump and then the sound of feet clambering against the wooden wall of the crap-house.

The smoke cleared and as Boy's eyes grew used to the darkness in the yard, he saw a shape at his feet. He knelt down and put his hand out.

It was Green, and he was dead. Boy could tell that immediately from the peculiar angle of his neck.

Boy was about to run, and then saw something glinting in the dark. His old magpie habits from his days on the street tugged at him. He prised the huge fist fully open and there, unharmed, was the music box.

He grabbed it and stuck it in his pocket. Then he heard the door to The Trumpet open behind him.

He jumped to his feet and sped away up the side alley that led to the street.

'Hey!' shouted a voice behind him. 'Hey!'

'The Phantom!' cried the voice as Boy disappeared. 'The Phantom has got Green!'

Boy did not stop. He simply ran, but as he ran it occurred to him that it was true. Green must have been struck by the Phantom, just as Boy was following him. It was a lucky escape. Any sooner and *he* might be dead too. Boy sped on, trying to ignore the fact that he had not got the information Valerian was after, and that now the source of that information was dead.

Boy ran madly, until finally he turned a corner and ran

slap into someone else. They fell together, flying into the mud of the street. Boy looked at the other runner, who lay sprawled across him.

It was Willow.

'Boy!' she screamed. 'Oh, Boy!'

She was in a state, Boy could see. She was gabbling, trying to find the right words to say.

'I saw – in his box–'

But she did not finish, because a figure suddenly rose up in front of them.

'In a hurry?' it asked.

They looked up to see a shadowy figure staring down at them. From his black cape, and extravagant red-plumed hat, they knew who the man was. This was the garb of a City Watchman.

Boy and Willow had different feelings on seeing the Watchman. Boy had spent much of his homeless years, the years before Valerian, trying to avoid the City Watchmen. In his opinion they spent far too long trying to capture hungry boys who had stolen food, and not enough stopping people killing each other in tavern brawls.

Willow, however, had just seen the body of her former employer hanging from the window of his private box.

'I'm so glad to see you!' she exclaimed.

'Yes,' said the Watchman sarcastically, 'I'm sure you are. Now, would you like to tell me whose blood that is?'

Boy looked at Willow and saw blood in her hair and across her shoulders. Then he noticed the Watchman was staring at *him*.

Boy looked at his legs, and noticed that he was covered in blood too.

Things were getting messy.

'I think you'd better come with me, don't you?'

48

Before either of them could answer he grabbed them both by the neck and dragged them away down the street.

Some way behind a tall figure followed, slipping in and out of the darknesses of the street.

13

Dawn had risen on the morning of December the 27th, and a pale light had stolen into the cell where Willow and Boy lay. The room was about six feet square, with solid stone walls and a single window with no glass but a closely spaced grid of iron bars instead. This let the cold in and stopped the prisoners from getting out, which was just what the Watchmen wanted. Cold prisoners were less trouble. They often died of exposure before anybody had to decide what to do with them, which saved a lot of trouble all round.

Willow and Boy lay on some sparse and dirty straw, trying to keep away from a hulk of a man who lay snoring next to one of the walls. He was huge. Once or twice he had rolled over and they had shivered on seeing his aggressive, scarred face. Fortunately he had so far shown no sign of waking up.

'Why don't they hurry up?' Willow asked again.

'We've got to get out,' said Boy again.

The window was high up, but by standing on Boy's shoulders Willow was able to peer out across the City below.

'I think it's going to snow today,' she said. For some reason it reminded her of when she was small, just a child, when she hadn't had to work to survive. On a day like that there had been a lovely, thick fall of snow, and she had played in it, carefree.

The sunrise was casting a pinkish light across the whole City. Mile after murderous mile of it stretched away as far as she could see. From high in the dungeon inside the Citadel of the City Watchmen the sprawl of buildings was laid out before her like a carpet. Even this early in the morning the City hummed and bustled with the noise of tradesmen up before the sun. In the gentle pink light, and from this height, the City looked almost beautiful to Willow. Almost. In recent years she had spent too long ducking and weaving her way through its narrow lanes and dark alleys to think of the place as beautiful. From where she teetered on Boy's back she could see a very long way. Could she even see the edge of the City, or was she just imagining it? Remembering it, maybe. A trip to the country when she was a little girl, with her parents. She told herself she was imagining it. She'd been too little when her parents had died to remember them.

'Have you ever been out of the City?' she asked Boy suddenly.

'Are you going to get down?' Boy asked back.

'Oh, sorry, yes.'

She slithered off his back and landed nimbly beside him.

'Thank you,' he said. 'Well?'

'I think it's going to snow.'

'The *window*, Willow?' he said.

'Oh, there's no way we're going anywhere. The bars are solid and besides, there's a drop that'd squash you flat. We're stuck.'

Boy slid back down into the straw.

'Then I'm as good as dead.'

'Korp *is* dead,' said Willow, and shivered again.

They were both silent.

'I don't even know your name,' said Willow after a while.

'Yes you do,' said Boy.

'What? Boy? That's just what he calls you, isn't it?'

She meant Valerian. Boy said nothing.

'That's your real name? Boy? That's not a name. You must have a real name.'

Boy looked at her.

'That's my *only* name. Before Valerian found me no one called me anything at all.'

Willow stared at Boy.

'So where did you come from?'

'I don't know.'

'You don't know?'

'No,' said Boy, beginning to wish he'd been arrested on his own.

'How can you not know? Where did you live before Valerian found you?'

'In the City.'

'Where?'

'Anywhere.'

'Always?'

'Yes,' said Boy. 'Is that so strange? Have you ever lived anywhere else?'

'No,' admitted Willow, 'but I know my name and I know I was born in the City, though I can't remember where.'

'And so do I,' said Boy angrily. 'My name's Boy and I was born in the City too! All right?'

Willow was quiet for a time, flicking her feet with a piece of straw.

'Sorry,' she said.

Boy mumbled something.

'Why are they taking so long?' she asked again.

'We've got to get out,' said Boy again.

There was a rattling of keys in the huge iron lock and the door swung back on its heavy hinges.

52

The Watchman who had locked them up several hours before ducked his head as he came back into the cell. He seemed surprised to see them. He glanced at the sleeping figure by the wall.

'Lucky for you he drank so much,' he said.

'Did you go and look?' asked Willow.

'Oh yes,' said the Watchman. His hat had a pink plume in it. This meant he was more important than the red-plumed one who'd arrested them. Willow thought this was a good sign, and would mean he could let them go. She'd told them about finding Korp and explained about the blood. She'd told them to go and see for themselves so they knew she was telling the truth. And Boy had just let them imagine that the blood on his clothes was the same blood that was on Willow.

'So you see that what we told you is true?' Willow asked.

'Oh yes. Very much so. And you will both be detained on suspicion of the murder of Director Korp of the Great Theatre.'

14

Valerian lurked in the shadows across the road from the Citadel of the City Watchmen. It was an old building, one of the very oldest in this very old city, and was a crazy mixture of styles and materials. Black-timbered box windows lurched unnecessarily far out of rough stone walls, doors halfway up walls led only to empty space, and ornate towers and spires twisted high into the early morning air above Valerian.

He hated being here, he disliked even being in this part of the City, which was a much richer and altogether *nicer* area than he was used to – than what he had *become* used to. The longest side of the Citadel overlooked the river and the stink coming from it was worse than ever. As if all that were not enough, it was daylight. Valerian could not remember the last time he had been outside during the day. It disturbed him.

It had all gone wrong, and time was running out. Had he really expected the boy to get the information he'd sent him for? And now he'd have to get Boy out of the Citadel, to know for sure that he hadn't. Valerian cursed under his breath. He didn't have time to be messing around like this.

Once, things had been so different for him, but as the last

54

few years had turned under his feet, the spectre of his past had risen to meet him like the dawn of a terrible day.

Well, there would be worse to come yet, that much Valerian knew for sure.

15

'This is not going well,' said Willow.

'I know,' said Boy, 'but what do you suggest?'

The figure in the straw stirred again. Very soon he might wake up, and with a significant hangover.

'Why did you tell them about Korp?' Boy asked Willow.

'I couldn't not, could I? I was covered in blood. I still am.'

She tried not to look at her clothes. It was bad enough that the stuff had now dried in her hair and matted together in places. She wanted a bath very much. Boy looked no better. For some reason he was wearing only sack-cloth leggings under his overcoat and from the knees down his legs were stained red-brown. Although Red-plume and Pink-plume thought this was Korp's blood too, Willow knew it was not.

'So tell me again how you've got blood on your legs. And where your clothes are. And what you were doing out at three in the morning.'

Boy sighed. Why did she always have to ask so many questions? He changed the subject.

'I can't believe Korp's dead,' he said.

'No,' Willow agreed.

'But that means . . .'

'What?'

'Well, the theatre. What will happen? There's no one to take it over and that means it will close and that means I'm out of a job.'

'Me too,' said Willow, 'but we don't know for sure it's going to close. Someone will take it over.'

'Who?' asked Boy.

'Well . . .' said Willow, thinking hard, 'Valerian?'

Boy was about to laugh, but then thought about it for a moment. Valerian was just about the only reason the Great Theatre was still going anyway. Why shouldn't he take it over? In fact . . . A terrible thought crossed his mind, but he pushed it away. There were other things to think about first. Besides, Valerian was utterly bored with the Theatre these days, only keeping the act going as a steady source of income.

'What will they do to us?' he asked Willow, but he knew the answer.

'Hang us, I expect.'

'Or drown us, maybe.'

They both fell silent again, contemplating a miserable end. The sun climbed higher over the City and shed a little light directly into their cell. Boy and Willow wasted no time in sitting in the patch of sunlight and at last they began to feel warm.

Boy shoved his hands deep into his pockets and his left struck something solid. He pulled out the music box. He turned it over. The only other time he'd seen one was in Kepler's house. He collected clockwork mechanisms of all kinds, and had once shown some to Boy.

Boy daydreamed, remembering the time a year or so ago when Kepler had come to stay in their house for a week while he installed the camera obscura. Even though he brought all the parts with him it had taken Kepler the whole week to fit it into the Tower room. There was a lot of banging and sawing and swearing during those seven days, but at the end Kepler had thrown open the door to the room.

'Behold!' he cried dramatically, and Valerian, who had not been allowed into his own chamber during the building, had entered. Boy had watched the door close behind them, and many months later was still none the wiser about what the machine actually did. As the door had closed, however, he had heard Valerian exclaim that Kepler was the Greatest Doctor of Natural Philosophies that had ever lived.

'What's that?' asked Willow.

Boy waved the music box at her and wound its handle a couple of times before putting it back in his pocket.

'I . . . found it,' he said. 'At The Trumpet. Listen to the music, because it may be the last we hear!'

'Oh, Boy, don't give up. It could be worse.'

'How could it be worse?' Boy asked, but Willow didn't answer, because the figure lying in the straw suddenly rolled over and vomited across the floor.

'Please get me out of here,' wailed Boy to no one in particular, and his prayer was answered.

The door rattled and opened for a third time, and Boy was amazed to see Valerian enter the room.

Before Boy could open his mouth, Valerian put his finger to his lips. Boy understood and said nothing and Valerian came into the cell, followed by Pink-plume.

'Two minutes,' he barked at Valerian, and then saw the mess on the floor. 'Or less, if you prefer.' He pulled a face and locked them in again.

Boy was pleased to see Valerian.

'How did–?'

58

'How did I know you were here? You don't think I'd trust you to get it right by yourself, do you? Something this important?'

Boy wished Valerian wouldn't talk like that, especially in front of Willow, but he was too relieved to care.

'Well?' said Valerian.

Boy said nothing.

'He wouldn't tell me anything. I–'

Valerian lurched forwards towards Boy, who flinched backwards, but did not hit him as he had expected.

'He's dead,' added Boy. 'Someone murdered him. Some thing. The Phantom.'

'What?' roared Valerian, then seemed to remember where they were and made an effort to calm himself.

'He's dead. He–'

'Not that! Did he tell you anything? What did he say before . . . ?'

'He wouldn't tell me anything,' Boy stammered. 'He–'

'Be quiet!' yelled Valerian, then quietened himself again. 'So he told you nothing before he died? Kepler sent him with information for me – the name of a grave. You're sure?'

Boy nodded, and Valerian flung his arms out wide, failing to find words bad enough to yell at Boy.

'I do have something,' Boy said. He fished in his pocket and pulled out the music box.

'That's it?' Valerian asked. 'Are you trying to be funny? I need a name, not trinkets!'

He stopped.

'Valerian?' asked Willow.

Only now did Valerian seem to notice her presence in the cell.

'Hmm?' he said, still staring at the music box.

'He said two minutes. Are you going to get us out of here?'

59

Boy cringed. This was not a good way to go about getting anything from his master. There was, in fact, no good way to get anything from him, but Willow didn't know that.

Valerian dragged his eyes away from the tiny mechanical object and shoved it in his pocket.

'I may as well leave you here,' he snarled. 'You are no use to me.'

'Please, Valerian,' Boy begged. 'It wasn't my fault he wouldn't talk to me.'

Valerian considered them both.

'All right then,' he said. 'I suppose so.'

He looked at Boy.

'Well, Boy, it's time you learnt the secret of the Fairyland Vanishing Illusion.'

'But that's just a trick,' said Boy.

'Ah!' said Valerian. 'No. In fact, the secret of the Fairyland Vanishing Illusion is that it is not an illusion at all.'

Boy stared at him. Willow stared at Boy.

'Boy . . .' she began, as keys rattled in the lock again.

'Quick!' commanded Valerian. 'Hold close to me.'

He grabbed them both and pressed them to his side.

Boy heard him muttering in some unknown language, and saw him pull something from one of his many pockets.

The door opened and Pink-plume stood in the doorway.

Valerian's arm swung through the air, throwing something.

'Ho!' he cried. 'Ho! And away to Fairyland!'

There was a huge rush of smoke and Boy lost all sense of where he was. He felt himself lurch upwards for a moment, as if flying.

Then the smoke began to clear.

'Run!' hissed Valerian.

60

Boy ran, and felt himself being pulled along by a hand he knew well. Valerian's.

They were in a stone corridor, somewhere in the Citadel. Willow was being pulled by Valerian too, and fast. He seemed to know exactly where he was going, and in a few more seconds they burst out on to a roof, high above the City.

'Come on!' Valerian shouted, and hurtled to the edge, pulling them both off after him.

'No!' screamed Boy.

They fell for what seemed like ages, but was measured by only a heartbeat and a half.

They hit the foul and freezing water of the river and, after another couple of heartbeats, surfaced spluttering and coughing quite near the bank.

'Come on!' urged Valerian, as he clambered out of the water by a small wooden jetty to which ferry boats were moored.

'Time we were gone,' he said. 'Besides,' he added, 'I hate daylight.'

Rolling them both into a ferry he climbed after them and pulled a dirty piece of canvas across them all. He set them adrift and they floated away downstream in the brisk current, heading for home.

'Are they following us?' Willow finally managed to splutter.

'No! They won't even know we're gone until the fool with the pink feather wakes up.'

Boy shook his head. He was used to not knowing what was going on, but this was worse than usual.

'Valerian,' he asked. 'Valerian, was that really magic?'

Boy had never believed that Valerian could actually do magic. Real magic. He was not sure he had changed his mind.

61

'Well, I got you out of the Citadel, didn't I? It must take real magic to do a thing like that, mustn't it?'

Boy lay shivering under the canvas. If it was magic, couldn't Valerian have got them straight home without having to swim in the freezing river? He was cold again, and wet this time too. He was soaked with stinking river water. At least he was back in a nice small dark space. He could cope with that. He decided to let the subject of magic drop. Let Valerian play his games. Boy had other things on his mind, like smoke. As they'd burst from the cell, there had been an awful lot of smoke. Purple smoke. Again. it was the second time in a few hours that Boy had seen purple smoke, and the first time had left Green with his throat cut and his neck broken.

What had Valerian said?

You don't think I'd trust you to get it right by yourself, do you?

Had Valerian been there all along, at The Trumpet? And Green – had Valerian seen to him too? No, he had wanted the precious information from Green. He wouldn't have killed him.

And Korp? Korp must have been killed about the same time that Green was, but the Phantom couldn't have been responsible for both. Boy tried to let the thoughts make sense so he could forget them, but they didn't. He worried.

The boat drifted downriver, back towards the Old Quarter where Valerian and Boy lived in their magnificent crumbling mansion.

16

By the time they made it back to the Yellow House, it was nearly midday.

Valerian slammed the door behind them.

Immediately he took the music box out of his pocket and glared at it.

'Kepler, where are you?' he said to himself. 'Where are you when I need you?'

Then he looked at Boy and Willow.

'Go and get cleaned up, Boy,' he said. 'I seem to say that a lot at the moment, don't I?'

'What are you doing here, girl?' he asked Willow. 'You can get cleaned up too and then leave.'

Valerian turned and made for the stairs to his own rooms.

'I think I had better get changed myself,' he said as he went.

Boy looked at Willow, then after Valerian.

'But where can she go? The theatre will probably have to shut. Korp's dead.'

'I know,' Valerian called back from halfway up the first flight of stairs, 'but this is not a doss-house.'

And he disappeared out of sight.

By the time Boy had found his smelly clothes from the night

63

before, and washed them and Willow's, and scrubbed his coat and boots again, it was getting dark.

Boy made a fire in the kitchen to dry all their wet things. They sat in front of it wrapped in blankets from Boy's bed, and shivered.

They had been listening to Valerian's curses and threats come floating down through the house all afternoon.

'You live here?' asked Willow, looking around her in wonder. The kitchen alone was vast, with unused implements and pots and pans hanging everywhere. The house must once have fed at least a dozen people every single day. 'Just you and him in this huge house?'

Boy nodded.

'But what are you? His slave?'

'No!' said Boy fiercely.

'Then he pays you?' asked Willow.

Boy hesitated before answering.

'No, but—'

'So you *are* his slave!'

'I am his famulus,' Boy cried.

Willow stopped.

'His what?' she asked.

'Famulus,' said Boy. 'His famulus. It means I attend him in his studies and investigations.'

'Is that what he told you?' Willow asked.

Boy said nothing.

'Isn't there anyone else?' Willow pressed. 'Who does the cooking? The cleaning?'

'I cook when he tells me to. No one does any cleaning.'

'But who taught you to wash clothes? To make fires? Someone must have shown you.'

'I don't know. He teaches me things, but not everyday things. I worked those out for myself.'

64

'And before you came here? Who are your parents?'

'I don't have any.'

'Neither do I, any more.'

'What happened to them?' Boy asked, wondering as he did so why he was bothering.

'They were killed,' Willow said. 'I was four.'

Boy was about to ask how they were killed, but Willow carried on before he could.

'My aunt put me in the orphanage,' she said.

'That was nice of her,' said Boy.

'She wasn't really my aunt. She was some old relative. I'm not sure what, exactly. But she couldn't look after me. Anyway, she died not long after that. I lived in an orphanage near the Palace walls until I got a job with the Liverymen. I was eleven then, four years ago. How old are you?'

'I don't know,' Boy said.

Girl looked at him, expecting some kind of explanation. Getting none, she carried on with her own story.

'Then I came to the theatre, but you know that,' she said. She looked hard at Boy. 'What about you?'

'What do you mean?' Boy asked.

'Your parents,' Willow said, sounding impatient.

'I said, I haven't got any.'

'I know that,' Willow said, 'but I mean, who were they?'

Boy shrugged. He knew she was only interested, but really, he wished she'd shut up.

'Look, I don't know. Since I can remember I just lived in the streets, freezing and starving in the winter, all right more or less in the summer. That's all there's ever been. Then he found me.'

Willow could see she was getting nowhere. She changed tack.

'He treats you like rubbish,' she said.

'At least I have a room and food and something to do.'

'That's not a room,' said Willow, remembering the box-like space at the end of the tunnel Boy had fetched the blankets from. She seemed stumped for anything to ask for a moment, then turned to Boy again.

'So who taught you to speak, then?' she asked.

Boy felt the clothes.

'They're dry, more or less,' he said, and Willow gave up.

They turned their backs to each other and dressed quickly. The clothes were warm from the fire and Boy began to feel better than he had for what seemed like a very long time.

'I'm hungry,' said Willow, 'Starving.'

'Let's see if there's some food here,' Boy said, but not very hopefully.

He was right to be pessimistic. He found some dried biscuits, and they ate them slowly.

'Boy,' said Willow suddenly, 'what about me?'

'You'll have to go back to the singer,' he said. 'You're not short of food there, at least.'

'But I can't!' Willow cried. 'I'm a wanted criminal! So are you, come to that.'

Boy hesitated.

'I know,' he said, 'I know. Look, I'll try and talk to Valerian again, see if you can stay. Then maybe you'll be safe from the Watch.'

'Would you?' asked Willow. 'Would you really?'

Boy looked at the hope in her face and felt himself shiver. He wasn't sure it was a good idea, for lots of reasons. And wasn't it like admitting she was guilty if she ran away? But something in him wanted her to stay.

He could *ask*, but the chances of Valerian agreeing were not good.

'Look,' he said, 'I'll try. That's all.'

'Why do you care?' said Willow.

Boy hesitated again. He didn't know that he did.

'I don't know,' he said.

They sat and watched the fire for a while, warming themselves while it lasted. Boy felt exhausted, as much by Willow's constant questions as anything. For the first time in years all sorts of thoughts crowded into his head. He pushed them away. He didn't need to know who his parents were. It wasn't important, no matter what Willow thought. Boy's thoughts became hazier.

Before they knew it, they had fallen asleep on each other's shoulders, and for a short time their weary bodies rested.

17

Darkness had fallen.

Boy and Willow woke up within moments of each other. They both got to their feet, avoiding each other's eyes.

'Well,' said Boy, looking at the floor.

'Yes,' said Willow. 'What do you think? Have you changed your mind?'

'No,' said Boy, looking up, and into Willow's eyes. 'Let's get it over with.'

They made their way up to the Tower room. After hours of hearing Valerian's rage and curses earlier in the day, it was quiet. It seemed as good a time as any to dare to ask him for favours.

Boy knocked on the door. That in itself was strange. Normally he waited to be summoned.

'What is it?' came the voice from within.

'Valerian,' called Boy, 'can we come in?'

There was a pause.

'We? Oh, very well.'

Inside Boy looked at Valerian, but not directly into his eyes. That was usually too much to take. Willow just stared and stared open-mouthed at all the stuff in the room – the vials, the jars, the machines, the devices, the equipment, the drawings, the books, the glass things, the brass things, the wooden things. The camera obscura.

'Why is she still here?' Valerian asked.

'Please, Valerian, can she stay? The Watchmen will be after her.'

And me too, he thought.

Valerian said nothing.

'And she can't go back to Madame, because the theatre will be shut and – oh!'

Boy stopped. The theatre.

'Yes,' said Valerian. 'I expect it will.'

'But that means we'll be out of work and–'

'I could not, at this moment, possibly care less,' said Valerian. 'And the girl cannot stay here. We have too much to do. That is an end to it.'

This stopped Boy in his tracks.

'But Korp is dead,' Willow protested. 'You'll have nowhere for your act!'

Valerian stood up, and Boy and Willow cowered where they stood. He seemed to tower above them, taller than ever.

'Listen to me. I do not care about the theatre or the act. The only thing that concerns me at the moment is time. Do you see?'

They both shook their heads, which seemed only to anger Valerian. Boy knew his moods well and shrank back against the wall of the Tower room.

'Listen to me! I am in trouble. Bigger trouble than failing theatres or dead directors. I now have four days left to save my life, and the only way I can do it is hidden from me! Green,' he waved the music box Boy had stolen from Green's dead hand, 'was supposed to give me a name – a name that could just possibly save my wretched cursed skin,

69

and yet I have been tricked! All I have is this worthless gimmick! How can this fairground rubbish give me a name?'

He threw it to the floor.

Willow stepped forward and picked it up. She held it to the light of the single lamp in the room and smiled. She turned the little metal crank and notes of music, tinny and small, rang out across the room.

'I know it does that,' snapped Valerian.

Willow ignored him. She had realised something about the music, which played again and again.

She listened to the tune. It was very simple, with only eight notes. A haunting refrain, and if Valerian had been more astute, he might have heard in it the chords of hope. Willow played it a few times, then a few more.

'Valerian,' she said, 'this is a name. This tune is a name, and the name you have been searching for is Gad Beebe.'

December 28th

The Day of
Worst Fortune

❧

1

After Willow had explained for the fourth time how she knew what the name was, Valerian began to believe it himself, and as he did so his mood suddenly improved.

'Music!' he exclaimed. 'Hidden in the music! Before my very ears!'

He laughed.

'Kepler knew what he was doing after all – he must have sent this thing for me. Green decided to play difficult and then . . .' He laughed again.

This worried Boy. He had never heard Valerian laugh before. It worried him a lot.

'And you learned this from Madame?' Valerian asked Willow.

She nodded. Yes, she had learned musical notation from Madame Beauchance. And more than that, the older woman had grudgingly told Willow that she had 'perfect pitch'. She could identify any note in isolation of any other note which might be used as a reference point – an ability it seemed Madame herself did not possess.

'And these notes – each one is a letter?'

Willow nodded again.

'G – A – D – B – E – E – B – E.'

'By chance the name uses only letters from the first seven

of the alphabet,' said Valerian. 'Whoever made this thing, or had it made, was not only musical, but had spotted this curious fact about Mr Beebe.'

Willow nodded again, Valerian laughed and Boy worried.

'Beebe,' wondered Valerian aloud. 'Beebe. I'm sure I know the name.'

'So,' ventured Willow, 'about me staying . . . just for a while.'

'Hmm?' said Valerian, his mind elsewhere. 'Hmm? Yes, that's – you might even be useful, unlike Boy.'

He held the music box mechanism in his hand, turning the handle, listening to the vital tune over and over again.

Then, at long last, the many clocks in the house began to strike midnight.

It was December the 28th.

As the last chime died away, Valerian's mood grew sombre again.

'Come,' he said gruffly. 'We have much to do and time is running out.'

Boy relaxed a little. He knew where he was with this Valerian.

2

The three figures stole through the unusually silent city streets. They had entered a Quarter where not many people came. It had not snowed, as Willow had thought it might. It was cold, however, and Boy was glad he had all his clothes on. Yet again he was out traipsing after Valerian. The only difference was that the girl, Willow, was with him this time.

'Put your boots back on,' Valerian had said.

'Again?' said Boy, but Valerian had ignored him.

Willow and Boy lagged behind the tall man as he strode rapidly down dark paths. The City was quiet. Partly it was the sudden cold snap that had sent people to their beds early, but mostly because Valerian was heading into one of the few pockets of the City that was somewhat deserted. This was the Black Quarter, where the last outbreaks of plague had broken out. As its inhabitants had fled the Quarter it had been sealed off by a ring of burning buildings until everyone left inside had survived or died. Although that was many years ago, people had been slow to move back into the Black Quarter, and as a result it was sparsely populated by only the very poorest citizens. The streets were much like any other, but even more dereliction was evident.

The buildings were dark, convoluted, tangled mazes thrown together over the years – crooked houses with slanted windows and warped frames. Between them ran the usual gutter-like streets, reeking and heaving with piles of filth. The three hurried on.

'What are we doing?' Willow panted to Boy, struggling to keep up.

'It's always like this,' Boy said. 'I never know anything. You'd better get used to it.'

But it wasn't always like this, Boy realised as soon as he said it. He was too out of breath to explain to Willow, but Valerian was different. Worse.

Boy was used to his moods, used to getting beaten, used to being ignored – but Valerian had definitely changed. Over the last few months he had become distracted. And now Boy knew why.

Four days to live.

Why?

What it was that was haunting Valerian remained obscured to Boy, but his master had been clear enough. Boy wondered if Valerian was deluding himself. How could he know he had only four days to live? Maybe Valerian had gone a little crazy and was convinced by some make-believe of his own invention.

But no. That would not be like Valerian.

Four days . . . That would take him to New Year's Eve, Boy realised. What could happen that Valerian could be so possessed by?

He had become obsessed. The stage act had become unimportant to Valerian – he had merely been going through the motions for a long time. That was why Boy had not been surprised when his meeting with Green turned out not to be anything to do with the act. Instead Valerian had been expecting a name – a name that he had been searching for.

It was still the first hour of December the 28th.

'Childermass,' Valerian had said quietly as he dropped the automatic latch on the door to the Yellow House.

'Sorry?' Boy had said.

Valerian glowered at them both.

'Childermass,' Valerian said, and began to walk. He called over his shoulder without looking back, 'Today is Childermass. The unluckiest day of the year.'

'Oh,' said Boy, looking at Willow, who opened her mouth to speak but said nothing.

They had trotted after Valerian, who was twenty long paces away already.

'Where do you think we are going?' Willow asked. Boy did not reply, but began to scratch his nose. Willow did not give up.

'Valerian!' she called.

Boy looked at her in alarm, for she still did not understand how to speak to Valerian, how to wait until he spoke to you.

'Valerian, where are we going?'

He did not turn round.

'Valerian!' she called, louder this time. 'Where are–'

And now Valerian was with them. Somehow he covered the paces from where he had been, and loomed over them in the deserted street. His eyes burnt through the darkness at Willow, and she began to shake. It was as if she was standing naked in a snowstorm – she felt cold and small and fragile. Valerian held her gaze until she finally pulled her eyes away and stared at the ground.

'Be quiet, Girl,' he hissed, 'or I'll leave you to rot here.'

He turned and strode off again.

'I told you,' said Boy. 'I told you. Don't upset him.'

He looked at Willow, then saw Valerian about to disappear down yet another shabby alleyway. He looked back at Willow. Her face was drawn and pale.

Boy put his hand on her shoulder.

'Come on.'

'How does he do that?' she asked.

Valerian had vanished around the corner.

Boy tugged at her arm anxiously.

'Come on,' he said. 'We're better off with him.'

Willow still didn't move.

'I know,' he said, 'I know what it's like. But really, it's best if we keep going. Stay with him.'

Willow nodded her head slowly.

'Where's he gone now?' he moaned. 'Come on, Willow. Please?'

At last she began to walk. Boy pulled her sleeve and she sped up slightly, but Boy knew that Valerian would be getting further ahead with every stride.

Valerian had gone down a small alley on the left, but now they were closer, Boy could see there were three of them leading off into even deeper darknesses, and he had no idea which one his master had taken. He scratched his nose.

The thought of being alone in the City at night worried him. It brought back memories of things he had half-forgotten, of all the years he had lived alone on the streets.

Boy hesitated, and the longer he hesitated, the further away Valerian would be getting.

Grabbing Willow by the hand he ran down the nearest alleyway, his boots plucking at the mud and filth underfoot.

'Valerian,' he called, but quietly. 'Valerian!'

It was so dark in the passage that he could barely see.

'Where is he?' Willow asked, still sounding shaken.

Boy kept running.

Suddenly they came out into a torchlit square. It was vast and empty. Beautiful old buildings leant inwards on all four sides, as if trying to get closer to each other across the cobbles that lay between them. Boy took in the square. Compared to the darkness of the alley, the light from the torches was amazingly bright.

There!

There was Valerian, unmistakable, about to disappear down a street that led off the far corner of the square.

Without a word Boy and Willow raced across the open space, feeling vulnerable and watched as they went. The City was quiet, and there still seemed to be no one else around. The sound of their boots on the cobbles of the square rang out like pistol shots.

They made it across and turned into the street Valerian had taken. Boy noticed the name of the street: The Dead-way. Another bad omen.

Valerian was waiting.

'You two make more noise than I care to hear,' he said as they arrived, panting heavily, but he waited for them to get their breath back without further comment.

'Right,' he said. 'Nearly there. Then our work begins.'

The look on his face was deadly serious. There was no anger or intimidation this time, none of his tricks of scaring the hearts out of them.

Just . . . thought Boy. *Just . . . fear?*

Could Valerian be scared? It seemed unlikely.

Valerian set off.

79

Boy looked at Willow.

'Are you all right now?' he asked as they followed.

She nodded, forcing a smile.

'I know,' Boy whispered. 'He's . . . difficult. But better the devil you know.'

Though Boy said this quietly, Valerian heard.

'What did you say, Boy?' he asked, though not angrily. 'A fair quote from you for once. But do not mention his name here.'

They had come to the end of The Deadway, and stopped.

Before them stood a huge pair of ornate bronze gates set into a long, high stone wall. The gates were covered in iron pictures of confusing and frightening design. Human figures, mostly naked, writhed and hung in peculiar postures and agonising angles from the bars of the gates. Here and there Boy and Willow could see less-than-human figures, but they were not in pain. They grinned demonically and held long sticks or poles or spears, with which they were pricking and piercing the bodies.

'What is this place?' Willow whispered, but Boy had understood.

'Look,' he said.

His voice was deathly. He pointed through the bars of the gates to where, beyond the walls, stretched row after row of cold, grey gravestones.

Above the gates was an arch, upon which were carved some strange words.

'What does that say?' Boy asked Valerian quietly.

'Is your reading still so bad?' Valerian sniped, but merely from habit. There was no life in his voice.

'But it's strange,' Boy protested.

'It's Latin,' Valerian said, 'and it's high time you learnt

some. *Mille habet mors portas quibus exeat vita. Unam inveniam.* It means, more or less, "Death has a thousand doors to let out life. I shall find one."'

3

It was bitterly cold. Boy and Willow were shivering, but not just from the temperature. Row after row of lifeless stones faded away around them into the darkness of the cemetery. They had crept inside through the massive iron gates, which were not locked. They could just make out shapes from the moonlight which slanted low over the wall of the cemetery. The land sloped slightly from where they stood, so that even in the darkness they could see the stones rising away from them. There were thousands, some small and plain, some big, some carved with complex designs. Some were not stones at all but impressive tombs made of huge blocks of stone, surrounded by spiked railings. They were designed to keep people out, though Boy thought how strange they looked, like cages, as if they were actually meant to keep people *in*.

'What are we doing here?' Willow whispered.

Boy shook his head.

'I don't know. He's just got a habit of finding unpleasant places to be.'

'Boy,' said Willow, 'If you don't ask him, I will.'

Boy looked at her, wondering if she'd learnt nothing from her recent experience of Valerian's moods.

'I mean it,' Willow said.

'All right!' he said. 'All right.'

Valerian stood a few paces away, trying to get his bearings in the endless death-field.

Boy approached slowly. Gingerly he tugged at the tall man's sleeve.

'Valerian,' he said.

'Ah! Boy!' Valerian said. 'Good. Now, take these.'

He pulled two candles from his pocket and a couple of large matches.

'There's not too much wind – we won't need lamps. I can almost smell it now! This *must* be the one.'

'Valerian,' Boy was firmer this time.

Valerian looked down at him distractedly.

'Yes, Boy, what is it?'

'What are we doing here?'

A shadow swept across Valerian's face, a flicker of rage.

'I don't have time to debate it, Boy! Don't you under-stand? Time is running out. Today is the twenty-eighth.'

'No, I don't understand,' shouted Boy, 'because you never tell me anything!'

Valerian clapped a hand across Boy's mouth and held it there.

Willow ran over, then stopped, seeing that Boy was not actually being harmed. She hesitated.

'How many times do I–' Valerian hissed. Willow stared at him. She saw the anger slip from his face.

'No,' he said quietly, and took his hand from Boy's mouth. Willow stepped to Boy's side and held his arm.

'No,' said Valerian again. 'You are right, Boy. I should tell you.'

Boy looked at him intently, waiting.

'I will tell you, but not now. There's no time now. First we must find it.'

83

'But what?' asked Boy.

'The grave. The grave of Gad Beebe. Isn't that obvious?'

No, it isn't, Boy thought, but he nodded. He smiled.

'That was what the music box told us?' asked Willow. 'To come here?'

'Yes,' said Valerian. 'Well, no, not exactly. I was looking for a grave, and now I have a name. We are looking for the grave of Gad Beebe, and this is the biggest cemetery in the City. We have to start somewhere!'

'And what then? When we find it? Why is it so important?'

'Later. We are running out of time. We'll find the grave first and then – damn!'

'What?' asked Boy.

'A spade. I forgot to bring a spade.'

Valerian stamped his foot and swore at the sky.

'Why do we need a spade?' asked Willow, but she and Boy had a terrible feeling they knew why.

'To dig his grave, of course. Never mind, there must be a sexton's hut here somewhere. The first thing is to find it. Now, let's get these candles alight . . .'

A succession of thoughts swept through Boy's mind, all of them ghastly. The news that was rife in the City about the Phantom and grave-robbers sprang to his mind. He looked at Valerian. Was it possible that he was the one who had been breaking into people's graves? Could Valerian be capable of such a thing?

Of course he could.

'No,' Boy said, 'I won't do it!'

Willow looked at Boy, surprised. Valerian too.

'What now?' he asked. 'Can't you see we must get on?'

'You can get on without me,' said Boy. 'I won't do it. I've done a lot of terrible things for you, but I won't do this.'

'Do what?' asked Valerian, the beginnings of a smile on his face.

'I won't steal people's bodies. People's . . . dead bodies.'

Valerian laughed. A short bark of a laugh. Then he shot a glance around him, and was silent.

'But Boy,' he smiled, 'we're not looking for a body! We're looking for a book.'

4

'Right. To save time, we'll split up. Here, take a candle each of you. Now, Boy, you go along this wall and work inwards, row by row. Work systematically and do not miss one out. Not one. You, Girl–'

'My name's Willow,' she said, then remembered that terrible look he had given her, 'sir.'

But Valerian was too busy thinking to care.

'Willow, go along the other wall. Do the same as Boy. Do not miss one out. I will go up this central avenue and work outwards. It's nearly the third hour after midnight. Meet back here in an hour. And remember – Gad Beebe. Inside his grave we will find the book, and then . . .'

His voice tailed off. He pulled a third candle from his pocket, and as much to amuse himself as to impress Boy and Willow, he pulled it out already alight.

'Can you teach me to do that?' asked Willow, but Valerian did not bother to reply.

Valerian went up the stony path that led into the dark heart of the cemetery, his small candle flickering in his hand, casting weak but unnerving shadows on the stones around him.

Boy and Willow looked at each other. They looked down the separate routes they were supposed to take, leading off into the pitch-black night.

'Book?' asked Willow. 'What's so important about a book?'

Boy shrugged.

'He's always going on about books, how important they are and why I have to learn to read better.'

'Maybe, but that's not enough of a reason to dig them up from graves, is it?'

'I don't know,' he said, 'but then I never do. I just do what Valerian tells me. Life's easier that way.'

Willow looked at him sadly, then she glanced down the rows of elaborate, ornamented graves, and shivered.

'Supposing', said Boy, 'we do half an hour my way and then half an hour your way? That would be about the same thing, wouldn't it?'

No, thought Willow, *it wouldn't*.

'Near enough,' she said, trying to sound bright. 'Anyway, if one of us holds the candles and the other does the reading, we'll be faster.'

'Yes,' said Boy, 'especially if you do the reading,' he added, shuffling slightly where he stood.

Willow smiled.

'Which way first?' she said.

Boy looked at the options.

'This way,' he said.

'Why?'

'No idea. Willow?'

'What?'

'How will we know when an hour has passed?'

'I have no idea. It's about as long as one of Madame's performances and one of Valerian's put together, but you know how time moves differently when you're doing . . . different things.'

'Yes,' agreed Boy.

He had a feeling this was going to be a very long hour.

Elsewhere in the cemetery, Valerian was thinking about time too. In his eyes, time was speeding up, every day, every hour. It seemed to him that every second lasted half the time of the one before, as if time was accelerating towards the end of the year. The end of the year, and the end . . .

He pushed the thought from his mind as he bent down to peer at the seventy-third gravestone he had looked at.

Trying to stay calm, he noted the name. Gad Beebe? No.

Gad Beebe? What kind of name was that? An important one. For Valerian it was a very important one.

What was today?

The twenty-eighth. Just three days left after today. Three days to find an answer, and so much depended on Kepler. Once, many years ago, he had trusted him completely, but things had changed. But he had always respected his learning, and now the stakes were high he needed all the help he could get.

Seventy-fourth. No.

Kepler. The camera obscura worked like a dream. It had cost everything Valerian had earned from the theatre for the last year, but it was worth it. Kepler had laughed at him when he'd first asked him to make it. What is the use? he'd scoffed. It will be of no use to you, at the end. It will not save you to see Fate approaching!

Seventy-fifth. No.

But then, when Valerian had persisted, he had changed his mind. Very well, he had said. Very well, I will waste your money. It will be expensive, he had said. I only make the best pieces of optical equipment.

Seventy-sixth. No.

And so they had agreed, and Valerian had slogged away at that stupid act for another year until the camera was built. Kepler had called him paranoid. Paranoid! He'd be paranoid himself, thought Valerian, if *his* time was running out. If something was coming for *him* he'd damn well be paranoid too!

Seventy-seventh. No.

Valerian straightened and moved on to the next stone, beginning to doubt he was going about this the right way. He knew there had to be a better answer, but just as an idea came into his head, his attention was caught by something up ahead.

A light.

There was a weak light flickering in the darkness ahead of him.

'That boy can't get anything right!' he cursed under his breath. 'I told him to stick to the wall.'

Valerian plucked another candle from his pocket and lit it from the one he was holding. No tricks this time. Pushing the candle into the earth of number seventy-eight to mark his place, he strode off to see what his boy was up to.

Approaching the source of the light, his eyes widened with surprise.

'Well! Hello, Valerian,' said a high, cracked voice.

Valerian turned to run, but a blow to the back of his head had him out cold before he even hit the ground.

5

'What?' whispered Boy.

'What?' replied Willow.

'What did you say?' Boy asked.

'I didn't say anything,' she said.

They were hunched over a grave. Yet another grave. They had been searching stone after stone, until the carved names had become a blur. Nowhere had there been a trace of anyone with a name even vaguely resembling that of Gad Beebe.

'What was that noise?'

'You're imagining things,' said Willow, as much to convince herself as anything.

'Isn't that an hour yet?' asked Boy.

'Yes,' she said. 'Yes, it must be. Come on, let's go back.'

'You are sure it's an hour?' Boy asked. 'I mean, we don't want to—'

At that moment there was another noise, the click of metal on metal, and although it came from a distance, they both heard it.

They froze.

'The candle!' Willow warned.

Boy blew the candle out. Utter blackness surrounded them. After a few moments they began to see a little as their eyes widened to catch as much light as possible. In the vague-grey shadow world, they suddenly both saw the same thing – a flicker of yellow light away to their left, in the heart of the cemetery.

'It must be Valerian,' said Willow.

'Why?'

'Well, who else would be out here?'

Boy didn't want to even think about the answer to that question.

'Yes,' he said, 'it must be. Come on. We may as well meet him there.'

They set off in the darkness and immediately Boy walked into a gravestone. The moonlight had vanished behind a bank of cloud and with no light to guide them the grey stones were as good as invisible. He picked himself up, silently cursing Valerian.

'Boy!' hissed Willow. 'Here's the path. Come on. When you get your feet on it you can follow the stones.'

She was right. By the feel and the sound of the grit underfoot they made their way more quickly towards the light. Boy found that by looking straight ahead rather than at his feet, he could see the faint grey ghost of the path better.

As they got near, something started to worry Boy.

'Willow?' he said quietly.

She ignored him. Either that or she hadn't heard him.

'Willow?' he said, stopping in his tracks.

She turned.

'Come on,' she complained. 'What is it now? I just want to go home.'

'Willow, I don't think that's Valerian.'

'Don't be difficult,' she said. 'Who else could it be?'

Her voice tailed off as she realised the double meaning of her words.

'And,' said Boy, 'Valerian went that way.'

Willow couldn't see the arm he waved in the darkness, but she understood.

For a long time they paused, uncertain what to do. The light was no more than a hundred feet away now and they could hear vague sounds coming to them across the stones.

'What if it *is* him?' Boy said.

'We'll have to go and see,' Willow said.

Boy pulled a face in the darkness.

'All right,' he said, 'but let's be careful. Please.'

Getting down on their hands and knees, they crawled the remaining distance between them and the light, leaving the path and cutting across the rows of small stones and larger memorials.

Boy could feel the damp of the scraggy grass begin to soak through to his knees. His hands pushed into patches of mud, cold but not yet frozen as it soon would as the winter hardened.

After a few minutes he could no longer feel his fingers; a little further and his hands had gone numb.

Still they pressed on, and as they neared the light and sound they saw they were right to have been cautious. It was obvious even from a distance that they were not the only ones working in the cemetery that night.

They came to a large tomb, with mourning angels surmounting the heavy stone cap, and decided to hide behind it. Peeping around the side of the grave, they had a clear view of an unholy scene.

Three men were hard at work in a grave. Around them lay various tools. Beside them a mound of earth spoil was piled on to a large sheet of canvas. A small glass lantern propped against a neighbouring gravestone illuminated the scene. The shadows it cast were long and grim. There was a spare shovel and an iron bar with a hooked end. And there was a large canvas bag with a lump inside it – a large, disturbing lump.

'Grave robbers!' hissed Willow in alarm.

Boy nodded.

There was no sign of Valerian.

'Come on,' said Boy.

Willow ignored him, trying to work out what was wrong with the scene.

The figures in front of them were shovelling earth back into the grave. It was obvious what was in the large sack next to them on the grass.

'Wait,' said Willow. 'Look. They're going. Let's wait.'

'Let's just find Valerian and get out of here.'

'In a minute. Look, they're going.'

It was true. The men worked fast and as soon as they had finished it took them no more than a second or two to gather their things, including the hideous bag, and leave. They swung away into the night, straight down the centre path of the cemetery, as bold as could be.

'He could never keep his nose out,' said one of the men. Boy and Willow started at the sound of his voice. It was high and wavered like that of a dying man.

Boy thought he heard another of them laugh, but maybe he was just imagining it.

Willow meanwhile had abandoned their hiding place and was scampering over to the grave.

Horrified, Boy hesitated by the tomb, unsure if it was more dangerous to follow or to stay where he was. Another glance behind at the yawning rows of death in the darkness persuaded him to move.

When he caught up with Willow she was crouching on the grass by the grave.

'Willow,' pleaded Boy, 'come on. Please. Let's just–'

'Look,' she said. 'You would hardly notice they'd been here. A bit of loose soil, but otherwise . . . just the grave, but then if it was a new one it would look like that anyway.'

She nodded at the fresh soil of the grave.

'Boy,' she said, 'what was wrong with what you just saw?'

Boy frowned at her, but it was wasted in the darkness.

'Apart from the fact they just stole some . . . body?' he asked, sarcastically.

'Exactly!' she said. 'They stole somebody. Well?'

Boy shook his head and looked around, expecting the grave robbers to return at any moment. He noticed a sickly light in the sky. It was still a fair time until dawn, but they could at least see more easily now.

'Look,' Willow said, 'I'm not an expert on the ways of resurrection men, but why would they fill the grave back up once they'd taken the . . . you know.'

'I don't know,' he said. 'All right, so it's strange, but could we find Valerian and discuss it at home?'

'Surely they'd just run – unless they needed to cover their tracks.'

'Or cover something up,' said Boy, despite himself.

'Or some . . . No, that's too horrible.'

They were silent as they stared at the freshly-turned soil at their feet. The daylight was coming stronger and faster now, casting weak light across the vast sprawling area of decay around them.

'Did you hear . . . ?' asked Willow suddenly.

Boy nodded, clenching his mouth tight shut and trying not to scream.

From the grave, just by their feet, they could hear a faint ticking sound. Faint but definite. It grew louder, became a knocking, regular and strong, then stopped.

94

Boy and Willow clutched each other. The noise started again.

Suddenly they understood, and both fell scratching and scrabbling madly at the loose pile of earth in front of them. The soil was not tightly packed but had already started to freeze in the cold morning air, and their hands were still numb and sore from their crawl across the cemetery.

They dug with claw-like hands until they were just paws of mud, scraping up fist after fist of grave-earth, until finally, gasping and straining, they reached the lid of the box.

It was broken. Of course it was broken, for it had already been broached earlier that night to release its horrible but valuable contents.

Were it not for this, they would not have saved him. In the time it would have taken them to find a pick or a chisel and smash their way clumsily into the coffin, he would have been dead.

As it was, it was a near thing. Their weak, failing hands barely managed to prise the broken portion of coffin lid out of the ground to reveal the choking, injured and terrified figure lying there.

Without a word, Boy and Willow fought the remaining soil to give up its prize. Boy began to pull at one of his arms, but as he did so a howl of pain ripped through the air. They put all their weight into pulling him up by his shoulders and then, at last, it was done.

Valerian lay coughing and spluttering on the mess of grass and earth beside the grave, half-dead, his right arm broken and hanging at a disgusting angle.

Next to him Boy and Willow crouched on all fours, panting like dogs, trying to breathe.

6

The journey back to the Yellow House was difficult and slow. Dawn had broken blue and bright before they were halfway back. It was hard going.

Boy was used to running and trotting after Valerian as he strode around the City, but now their roles were reversed. Boy and Willow had to lead him cautiously back through the twisting streets. He stopped frequently, the pain from his broken arm coming in surges, overwhelming him. They had tied the end of his right sleeve to the collar of his coat, in an attempt to fashion a sling to stop him from doing his arm more damage, but it was far from perfect. Willow had nearly been sick as they had moved Valerian's arm back into something like the right position, and he had screamed with pain more than once.

Boy's mind raced. Who had done this to Valerian? Someone had buried him alive – the man with the cracked voice and the others. Was it just because he had disturbed them at their grave-robbing? Nothing made sense.

Boy feared for the future. Valerian was difficult, unpleasant, violent and sour, but at least he kept Boy safe, more or less. Now here Boy was leading *him* back home.

'Nearly there, are we, Boy?' he would ask. 'Nearly there?'

Boy shuddered. They were nowhere near home yet. Why didn't Valerian know that?

But at last they were leaning Valerian against the posts of the outer doors of the Yellow House.

'Pocket,' mumbled Valerian, unable to say any more.

Boy fumbled in Valerian's right-hand pocket until he found his big bunch of heavy keys.

It took Boy a while to find the right one – a sudden clumsiness overtook him as he listened to Willow trying to soothe Valerian.

'Just a minute more, Valerian,' she was saying, 'and we'll get you into bed. You need to rest.'

Finally Boy turned the tumblers of the lock and they half-dragged Valerian inside.

It seemed to take the last of Valerian's strength to get upstairs to the first floor, where his bedrooms were. Even then Boy and Willow had to do their best to lift him up each of the ancient wooden stairs and then along the corridor.

They sat him on the bed and pulled his boots off. When they stood up, the huge man had passed out on the covers. They could not move him any more.

'What about this?' asked Willow, holding up a blanket she had found in a box at the foot of the bed.

Boy nodded.

They covered him up with the deep red quilted blanket and stood back.

'What are we going to do?' asked Willow quietly.

Boy said nothing.

'A doctor,' Willow went on. 'We must fetch a doctor.'

Boy hesitated.

'I don't know,' he said, 'He hates anyone coming here. He hates doctors. He hates interference.'

'But he's in trouble. And we can't do anything.'

'There's only Kepler. I don't even know if he's a real doctor, but–'

'You must go and get him,' said Willow firmly. 'You must get him to come and mend Valerian's arm.'

'Now?'

'Yes.'

'But it's early still. Willow, it's early and I haven't had any sleep. I can't go now. Look at me! Look at us.'

They were still covered in grime and mud from the cemetery.

'Please, Willow,' said Boy, 'I'm so tired . . .'

At the mention of this word, Willow felt her energy slip away.

'Well, he's safe enough for now, I suppose,' she said, looking down at where Valerian lay sprawled across the bed.

She went and sat by him, and then put out a hand to gently touch his forehead. He didn't react, but he was breathing.

'I'll go,' said Boy, sitting down on the bed too. 'Just let me have a little sleep first.'

He looked at his master and felt a rush of panic clear his tiredness for a moment.

'Valerian! Valerian!' he whispered, but there was no response.

Glancing away he saw that Willow had dropped off to sleep beside him.

Boy put his head on the covers next to hers and they slept deep, but troubled, sleep.

Boy woke screaming, waving his arms out in front of him, pushing at a coffin lid he thought was closing him away from the light for ever.

With his hands still covered in the soil from the grave it was all too easy to dream that it was he and not Valerian who had nearly been buried alive. What a way to kill someone! Boy thought.

He gazed around.

Valerian's room. He remembered bits of the night before. He felt like crying, but tears would not come.

Willow lay snoring softly, tucked in against Valerian's side like a kitten with its mother.

Valerian had not moved from where he lay on his back, more unconscious than asleep, Boy guessed.

And then Valerian spoke.

'Coming!' he said. 'It's coming . . .'

Boy jerked upright. He had never heard anyone talk in their sleep before. He stared at Valerian.

'It's coming!' Valerian mumbled again, barely opening his mouth. The words were slurred and unclear, but they did not stop.

'Time! What's the time? Boy, where are you?'

'Here!' Boy said urgently. 'Valerian, I'm here!'

But Valerian was not listening, only talking.

'Time . . . running out now . . . when? What's the day, today . . . Boy . . . time . . . it's coming.'

Boy tried again to reach Valerian.

'What's coming, Valerian?' he asked.

'Time,' said Valerian.

Was that an answer?

'What's coming? What's the matter?'

'Time is coming. The time is coming,' said Valerian.

'What's the matter, Valerian? What's happening to you?' Boy persisted, desperate now.

'The time . . . time coming . . . the book! Must . . . the book! Oh please . . . the book . . . The Eve of the Year . . .'

The book again! Boy knelt over Valerian, trying to catch every word, but as he did so a knocking from the front door made him jump. No one ever came to the house – no one unexpected. No one called to see Valerian without having been summoned by Boy. Even then Boy could only remember Kepler visiting.

For a moment he thought he might have imagined the sound, but it came again, louder this time. Someone was definitely there.

'Open up!' came a shout from the street.

Boy left the bedroom and ran lightly down the corridor to a small leaded window that looked over the front of the house and down on to the street.

He could just see a red feather.

His heart began to race.

The knocking on the door resumed, louder than ever.

He ran on tiptoe back to the bedroom and found Willow awake and blinking in the strong light of late morning.

'What is it?' she asked. 'What's that noise?'

'Watchmen outside!' hissed Boy, his eyes wide.

100

She nodded.

'Go and hide in my room,' said Boy. 'I'll get rid of them.'

'How? Don't be stupid! We must run!'

'We can't!' Boy said, pointing at Valerian.

'We'll just have to wait until they've gone away.'

'*If* they go away,' said Boy.

They cowered on the bed, not knowing whether to hide or run. They listened to the knocking on the door getting louder and louder, just as their hearts were thumping harder and harder in their chests.

'Open up! We demand you open up!'

'They know we're here,' hissed Willow.

'Maybe,' Boy whispered back, 'maybe not. Just don't move.'

'Open up! Persons in this house are wanted on suspicion of murder!'

Boy put out his hand to stop Willow from speaking.

'I don't think they know that we're here. Just wait.'

The banging on the door went on for another few minutes, and then stopped.

Willow made to get up from the bed, but Boy waved her to sit down.

'Wait,' he mouthed.

Sure enough, a moment later there was another banging on the door. They waited for it to stop, and finally it did. Boy made Willow sit still for nearly five more minutes before he got up and crept to the window.

'They've gone, I think,' he said. 'We've got to leave before they come back.'

'But supposing they've left someone watching the house?' Willow cried.

'What is all this noise?'

Boy and Willow turned and stared.

Valerian stood by the bed.

He looked like death. His clothes were covered in grave-soil, his hair stuck up at stupid angles, and his right arm hung limply by his side, having loosed itself from the makeshift sling.

'Valerian!' cried Boy.

'Boy, be quiet! I can't stand you shouting and wailing all the time! I want quiet!'

Valerian swung his good arm in front of him wildly. He fumbled in his inside pocket and pulled something out, which he raised to his lips. He tipped his head back and drank, then threw the object to the floor.

It was a small glass bottle, not much larger than a phial. Valerian wiped the back of his left hand across his lips and looked at the pair of them. He saw them looking at the bottle on the floor.

'For the pain,' he explained. 'One of Kepler's more useful concoctions.'

'But your arm!' Boy said.

'Is broken. Yes,' said Valerian. 'But there are more important things to deal with.'

'Who was that,' Boy asked, 'in the cemetery? Who did that to you?'

Valerian ignored him.

'We have much to do, and time is running short.'

'I don't believe you!' shouted Willow, breaking her silence. 'I don't believe you! You have us crawling around that death-field all night, hunting for some stupid book. You're practically buried alive and we dig you out with our bare hands and drag you home! And you won't even tell us what it's about! I hate you!'

Boy turned in horror to Willow, and when she had finished, he shook her by the arm.

'She doesn't mean it, Valerian,' Boy said. 'She's just tired and we don't need to–'

But Valerian held up his hand, his only good hand.

'No,' he said, 'the girl is right. It is time to tell you, but we must act fast. I was a fool last night. I thought once I had the name it would be a simple thing to find the grave where the book . . . and then . . . And then I was a fool to risk the cemetery. Those were old acquaintances of mine. I owe them money – quite a lot of money for some things they obtained for me once upon a time. Never mind that now, I must be brief. They seemed to think that putting me in the earth was an appropriate way of settling our differences.'

'But–'

'Listen. I am alive. I want to stay that way. And on the Eve of New Year I will face something much worse than a few grubby resurrection men, unless I can find a way out.'

They nodded.

'I need your help,' said Valerian and then, looking at his broken arm, 'more than ever now.'

8

'What's her name?' Valerian asked Boy.

'Her name is Willow,' she said crossly.

'Willow,' said Valerian. 'Willow, would you go to the Tower and get as many of those as you can find?'

He pointed with his foot at the empty bottle on the wooden floor.

'They're in a cupboard by the narrow window. Boy, where are my keys? Quickly! We have no time to lose.'

Boy found the keys on the floor of Valerian's bedroom where he had dropped them.

'Here,' said Valerian, giving the key to the Tower to Willow.

Boy stared. Valerian was actually giving one of his keys to someone else. To a girl he barely knew! Boy had never had possession of any of his keys before early that morning when he'd plucked them from Valerian's deep pocket.

Willow ran off to the Tower.

'Now, Boy, I need you to do something for me. I wasted time by hunting round the cemetery at random. Why?'

'Because it was too big', ventured Boy, 'and too dark?'

'Partly,' said Valerian, 'but something else too. Do you suppose that's the only cemetery in the City?'

Boy understood.

'You don't even know which cemetery he's buried in? Beebe?'

'Exactly. We were in the largest one, but there are others. And what else?'

Boy thought hard. There were cemeteries and then there were . . . churches!

'Church graveyards!'

'Good!' cried Valerian. 'And have you any idea how many churches and how many churchyards there are in the City?'

Boy thought.

'A dozen?' he asked.

'A hundred and seven. And how long is it going to take us to look through them all?'

Boy thought hard again.

'A very long time?'

'No,' said Valerian, 'it's not going to take us any time at all, because we're not going to look. We're going to find out exactly where Gad Beebe is buried first. I need you to visit someone – the Master of City Burials. I should have done this before, only . . . he's an awkward man.'

'Is he a friend of yours?' asked Boy.

Valerian frowned.

'I know him. At least I used to, in my days at the Academy. He is the only source of cadavers for dissection in the City. Well, the only official source.'

Valerian saw the question on Boy's lips.

'Work it out, Boy! Would it be clearer if I said "bodies to cut up"? To study the nature of the human organism. So I had a few dealings with him until I . . . left . . . academia. There's a building in The Reach that's his official residence. Go there and tell him Valerian sent you. Tell him I need to know the whereabouts of a grave.'

Boy knew The Reach. It was a rich part of town. Before

Valerian had found him, he had often spent summer days there, begging and, when no one was being generous, picking pockets.

'You must go there and get the location of Beebe's burial. All burials that occur in the City are recorded there. All official ones, that is.'

Valerian brushed at the dirt on his coat.

Boy thought about it for a moment.

'What will you do?' he asked.

A look of irritation crossed Valerian's face, but it passed.

'The girl – Willow and I will go to Kepler. I need him to mend my arm. I need someone to help me. I also need someone to go to the Master of Burials, and that will be you. You know the way there and Willow does not. Meet us back here this evening. Only enter the house after dark, light no lights and answer the door to no one. The place is safe enough.'

'How will I get in if I get back first?'

Boy thought about the shock he'd had the time he'd tried to pick the lock.

Valerian smiled.

'It's time you had your own key.'

He pulled a key from the bunch and handed it to Boy.

'The only spare. Don't lose it. Now, back here after dark with the name of the cemetery. Understand?'

Boy nodded, as usual.

'Then go! And do not fail!'

Boy turned to go.

'Valerian.'

'What is it?'

'You said he was awkward. The Master of Burials. What do you mean?'

'He is cantankerous. Prone to strange moods. And difficult to work with, too. When I last knew him he had become involved in some studies of his own. I never found out what. It made it impossible to get what we needed from him any more, and we had to use . . . alternative sources. That's all.'

Boy hesitated still.

'You have nothing to fear! Now, go!' Valerian said, and pushed Boy towards the door.

Boy fled from the house, clutching his key, without even telling Willow where he was going. And this time Valerian would not be there to get him out of trouble.

9

It was long past noon. Boy trotted along the streets, out of habit keeping to the shadows and smaller alleys. He had never liked being on his own, and with the thought of those feather-brained, feather-hatted Watchmen on the lookout for him too, he felt more timid than usual.

It was December the 28th. The sky was clear and ice-blue. Columns of grey smoke twisted feebly up to meet it from chimneys and other funnels on the rooftops. It was still cold, if anything colder than it had yet been all winter, but there was still no sign of the snow that Willow had sensed.

It was a busy day, with people going about their business in the street and behind doors.

Boy had not even had time to clean his hands, and as he made his way along the streets he picked at the soil stuck to his fingers. It gave him the creeps.

He had entered a dream-world. Two days ago everything had been normal, or as normal as life ever was with Valerian.

But everything had changed. Although Boy knew that things had started to change for Valerian months ago, it seemed to be coming to a head now, in these last days of the year.

The festivities and celebrations were over, for the time being, until another burst of frenetic fun at New Year. The

City had been a riot of noise and rare winter colour up to the 25th. Despite the poverty that most people struggled against, they somehow saved and hoarded all the little luxuries they could for the mid-winter feast. Maybe some rare dried fruit, some decent wine or strong beer was all it took to warm their hearts for a few days, reminding them that winter could not last for ever, that spring would return eventually, bursting green and golden. For those very few of the City who were rich, it was a time of greater indulgence and the giving and receiving of gifts, but the purpose of the festivities was just the same, creating a candle-bright haven in the depths of winter.

Now, in the few days before the New Year arrived, there was a lull. It was an unusual time, Boy thought, and he knew he had always felt this. Even in the days before Valerian, the days on his own, when he had lived like a mouse in the hidden nooks and crannies of the City, he had always felt these few days before the New Year to be different from the rest. This interlude was a strange and quiet time, a time somehow outside the rest of the year, outside time itself. It was as if the rest of the year were alive, but these days were dead.

Boy was not surprised that if he *had* entered a dream-world, it had happened during the dead days.

He had had barely any sleep – perhaps that was adding to his sense of the unreal. But it was true that he had been in a prison cell, under suspicion of involvement in the murder of his – and Valerian's – former employer. Korp had been spread all over the box where Boy had spent whatever free time he could. Willow and Boy had been incarcerated in the Watchmen's Citadel, and Valerian had effected a daring escape. They had spent a night crawling around a cemetery looking not for a body, but for a book. Surely a library was the place to look for a book? And he and Willow had then pulled his master half-alive from a freshly-robbed grave.

This was not normal, even for life with Valerian. And Valerian had told them there was worse to come. Nothing Boy knew, or had ever known about Valerian made him doubt it.

Boy trotted along through the City, grim resolution on his face.

10

'Where did you find him?' asked Willow.

'Do you always ask so many questions?' said Valerian, irritated.

'Only when I want to know something,' she said. 'So where did you find him?'

Valerian and Willow were slowly making their way to see Kepler. Willow kept forgetting the reason for their visit, kept forgetting that Valerian's arm was broken. The drug – whatever it was he had taken in the house – was doing a remarkable job of shielding him from the pain. Willow had retied his arm in something much more like a proper sling, and tucked the loose sleeve of his long dark coat into its pocket.

'You wouldn't even know there was anything wrong,' she had said, 'unless you looked hard.'

'I can tell you there's something wrong,' said Valerian, and took a small swig from one of the bottles Willow had found in the cupboard.

'Well?' Willow pressed, but gently. 'Where did you find him?'

Valerian looked down sideways at her, narrowing his eyes, but he was too sleepy from the drug to be really annoyed. He began to talk.

'Boy fell from the sky,' he said, 'sort of. In a church. I was

111

in a church – not something I make a habit of, but it was raining hard and it was somewhere dry, if not warm. And he was in one of his hiding places. I think he had lots of them. He's good at getting into small spaces – that's why I thought he'd be good for the act. Anyway, I was talking to . . . well, Korp, as it happens. Our dear departed Director. We had arranged to meet to discuss the act. And the next moment Boy fell on top of me, more or less. Here, we need to take that street over there.'

Valerian nodded and Willow steered them on their way.

'That can't be all, Valerian,' she said. 'Why does he live with you? What did he do before?'

'I don't know what he did before. He lived on the streets. He says he can't remember a time before that. He could speak, though, so he must have grown up with people somewhere or other.'

Willow nodded thoughtfully.

'And I taught him to read, though he is a terribly lazy scholar . . .'

Did she imagine it, or was there a slight softness in Valerian's voice?

'It must have been hard for him,' said Willow, trying to get Valerian to tell her more.

'What?' he snapped.

'Living by himself. In the City. That must have been hard.'

Valerian snorted.

'Maybe so, but he'd do better if he paid me more attention. It doesn't matter. The point is, he came to live with me. I had started to work at the theatre, being short of money, but although I had created an act, I needed help. I needed someone to be mine – someone who would do exactly what I told them without questioning why. Someone

I could trust. Boy's arrival was like a foretold event. It was meant to be, you see.'

'Not really,' said Willow.

'Well, there I was talking to Korp about my state of health, and the act, and the fact that I was nearly ready but just had to find the right assistant, and then . . . there he was. At my feet.'

'I see,' said Willow.

'And do you know, in a strange way I knew straight away he was the one. It was as though we had always been together. It works.'

'So why are you so hard on him?' asked Willow.

'I am not hard on him,' said Valerian. 'He needs a firm, guiding hand. He is prone to laziness and stupidity.'

Willow thought about defending Boy, but sensed Valerian's mood. She changed the subject.

'So why did he fall from his hiding place, then?'

'He said it was what I was saying.'

'What was that?'

'As I recall, I was explaining to Korp why I needed – why I had decided to create the act for the theatre. I was running short of . . . money. As a result of which, a . . . few problems had left me in a state of some ill health. A doctor was called. The doctor pronounced me either dead or dangerously sick. I understand it was those words that surprised Boy into relinquishing his grip on the stones.'

Willow frowned.

' "Dead or dangerously sick"?' she asked. 'What does that mean?'

'Well, I think Boy was as confused as you. This is, however, where I get my mistrust of doctors in general. The man was a charlatan, and nothing he did had the slightest to do with my survival and recovery.'

113

'And Kepler?' asked Willow, thinking of the doctor they were about to meet.

'Kepler is no ordinary doctor. In fact, Kepler is no ordinary man, and will do the best that can be done for my arm.'

A mile or two across the City Boy was nearing his destination – the wide and relatively clean street known as The Reach. Halfway along it lay the official residence of the Master of City Burials. Like many of the organisations that ran various aspects of City life, that of City Burials was a little strange. Like the others it operated from the official house of its Master. Each one was a small governance in its own right, with its own set of laws and rules and those in charge giving orders to those who obeyed, with the Master himself at the top.

Each was housed in a grand building, a reminder of the City's ancient and proud past. Some were now more than a little the worse for wear, according to the prosperity of the Chamber or Society that operated from them.

Of course, all these organisations were ultimately ruled by the Emperor, but in practice no one knew much about this. Emperor Frederick was a strange and remote figure, hidden away in the Palace. Something of a city within the City itself, the Palace occupied a vast area atop a low hill near the banks of the river. It was composed of a huge variety of buildings of various ages and styles clambering over one another for supremacy, and all surrounded by a high, crenellated wall. The title Emperor was something of a joke

– a pathetic hangover from the days when the City had been ruled by a leader of awesome power, when there had actually been an Empire to rule, of which the City was its magnificent capital. Not any more. Gone was the Empire, gone was the power and the magnificence of the City, and all that was left was Frederick, the last of his line, with no offspring to rule after him.

It was more than ten years since anyone outside the Palace had seen Frederick, and only then by accident. Life in the City functioned largely without him.

The building which housed City Burials was splendid and wealthy. Death was always good business, and since the Master's men co-ordinated all aspects of a person's life after death, from mortuary services to undertaking to burial and funerary rites, he was very wealthy indeed.

Boy stood on the other side of The Reach in a doorway opposite the ornate building. It stood imposingly, its front doors up a flight of at least a dozen stone steps, each door three times Boy's height, heavy and solid. On them hung huge polished door knockers, shaped like lions' heads.

There was an inscription in the stone above the doors.

'Latin, I suppose, Valerian,' Boy said to himself, and smiled. Then the smile drifted from his face. Valerian was in trouble. It was more than just a broken arm and it was up to Boy to find the solution.

He swallowed, looked up and down the street, and crossed. He skipped nimbly up the stone steps and, reaching up on tiptoe, swung one of the lions against its base.

The loud metal clunk seemed to echo the length of the street, but as Boy looked around nervously he was relieved to see that no one was paying him any attention. Nor, unfortunately, did anyone inside the building seem to have heard.

He swung the lion harder and waited.

'Side entrance,' said a voice beside him.

Startled, Boy looked to his right and noticed a small hatch set in the soaring pillars between which the doors remained implacably shut. Inside the pillar was a tiny room in which sat an incredibly small old woman, with a wrinkled face and an expression to match.

'Come about a death, have you? Round the side.'

'Yes – no – not exactly.'

The woman was unimpressed.

'Death? Round the side. Side door, see? That's where you register.'

Boy was puzzled.

'Then what do *you* do?' he asked.

'Well,' she said, 'I tell people about the side door.'

'That's it?' Boy asked. 'That's all you do?'

'It's important. Someone's got to tell people about the side door. For deaths. Important,' she added.

'And I wonder', he said, 'who tells me where to go if I haven't got a death to register.'

The woman looked blankly at him. She blinked.

'Well,' she said, peering anxiously around before answering, 'well, I could, probably, tell you.'

'Oh good,' said Boy. 'So where do I go to speak to the Master of City Burials?'

'Well, then you'd want to knock on the front door there and . . . *what?*' She spluttered to a stop. 'What do you mean? Don't waste my time!'

'No,' said Boy earnestly. 'No, I really need to see him. My master sent me – his name's Valerian. He said to say he sent me. We have to find out where someone is buried.'

'You can't see him. You think proles like you just wander in off the street for a chat?'

'But look,' he said, 'the thing is, Valerian, he's a friend of the Master. And he needs to find out something, about where a grave is—'

'Listen to me,' she said. 'Listen. No one gets to see him.'

'But I have to see him!' cried Boy.

'No!' snapped the woman. 'He's very busy working on his animals in the Dome. He won't think about anything else. No one talks to him.'

'What's he doing with animals? Doesn't he have lots of work to do for the cemeteries and so on?'

'Well, I don't know, of course, but he's been working in the Dome with his animals for years and it must be very important because he is the Master and it must have lots to do with burying people or he wouldn't be doing it.'

Boy was puzzled, but he nodded anyway.

'What is he doing with them?' he asked. 'What are the animals for?'

'Well, nothing much. They're dead, you see.'

A creeping little curiosity inside Boy told him he was going to have to find out what the Master of City Burials was doing before he went back to Valerian.

12

This was something Boy was good at.

Creeping and climbing around the dark spaces of buildings that no one even knew existed was something he had always done. Even Valerian had to admit that Boy was very good at not being seen.

Standing back in the street he had immediately spotted what he assumed must be the Dome the woman had spoken of. It was a huge glass roof made of hundreds, probably thousands, of individual panes of glass. They arched in a single beautiful sweep from some part of the building out of sight from where Boy looked. He'd spent a long time stalking the area, and now dusk was coming. In the half-light, the dome shone with the light of a thousand torches – or so it seemed to Boy. It was a glowing, shining, crystalline bubble that gleamed out of the filth of the City like a diamond in a dungheap.

Boy had scouted around the streets that joined The Reach, and found a small alley running into the centre of the block. There was a narrow but sturdy iron gate across the entrance to the alley, but Boy was over it before he had even wondered what he was doing. If he had stopped to think, he might have noticed that he was actually enjoying himself. This was like home to him. It was familiar ground –

running, climbing, hiding in the dark, with a mission to perform for Valerian. It was almost like normal.

He skipped down the alley as lightly as a rat, realising as he went that the alley was some kind of rubbish heap for all the buildings that ran behind it. Walls rose up high on either side of him, but just as he expected, there were little gates into the back courtyards of each building.

Accurately, he guessed where the gate for the Burials building would be.

There beyond lay the Dome, and for the first time he could see the stone building that it rose from. In a way he was disappointed that the shining glass roof rested on anything at all – it was so magical it ought to have floated in the air.

He looked to the gate. No way to climb over this one – it was set into the solid stone wall, but he had his bent metal pin out of his pocket and into the lock in a moment.

The gate swung and then he ran, quickly but cautiously, to the base of the Dome.

Some elaborate block work made climbing the building as easy as walking up stairs, and soon he was crouching against the glowing glass of the Dome itself.

He looked down at what lay within, and his jaw dropped. He had listened intently to what the old woman in the pillar had said about the Master of Burials and his animals, but nothing could have prepared him for what he saw now.

13

Dusk was settling over the winter cityscape as Valerian and Willow got to Kepler's house. On the way Valerian chatted almost casually to Willow, mostly about Kepler, about how he had been born of a noble family, but had turned his back on his aristocratic lineage for the pursuit of knowledge. Valerian looked up at the darkening sky.

'The end of the 28th,' said Valerian mournfully. 'Three days . . .'

Valerian rang the bell. Kepler's house was by no means as large as Valerian's, but was in a far better state of repair. This was a much cosier neighbourhood, of terraced houses for the well-to-do if not the rich. Kepler's house was a narrow, but tall affair.

'No light within,' said Valerian, frowning.

'Shall I knock?' asked Willow, but Valerian put out his good hand to stop her.

'He must be out,' said Valerian, but there was no certainty in his voice, 'but . . . he goes out no more than I do. Try the bell again.'

As Willow stepped forward, she noticed something else.

'Valerian!' she whispered. 'The door is open!'

'Careful, child,' said Valerian, but he did not stop her.

Valerian shoved the door further open with his boot, and they listened hard for a minute or so. The street behind them was empty and quiet. They took two steps into the hall and then pushed the door shut behind them.

'Kepler!' hissed Valerian in a stage whisper. 'Kepler, are you there?'

There seemed to be no one in the house.

'I think we can risk a little light.'

Willow started to hunt in her pockets for a match but was puzzled to see Valerian step over to the wall.

He found what he was after, and turned a small metal knob set into the wall itself.

Immediately a dim, flickering light sprang up in a chandelier above their heads.

Willow let out a small shriek.

'Valerian! Your magic *is* real!' she cried.

'No, Willow, no,' said Valerian. 'This is not my magic, but Kepler's genius. He has greater knowledge than anyone in the world of electrical phenomena. He has installed an automatic system of electrical light in his home. He says one day all houses in the City will have the same. He's mad, of course, but you have to admire his invention. My simple chemical lights at the theatre are child's toys compared to this.'

Valerian walked into a room leading off the back of the hall and turned another knob, throwing light across what was clearly Kepler's study.

Willow followed, open-mouthed.

'There's a large array of electrical cells in the cellar,' explained Valerian, but this was lost on Willow. She marvelled at the lights on the walls.

'There's no flame!' she said with disbelief.

'No,' said Valerian, 'but please concentrate.'

'Where is he?' asked Willow, dragging her gaze away from the magical lights.

'We must search the house. Something is wrong.'

Valerian winced as he spoke.

'Damn this arm!' he moaned. He rummaged in his deep left-hand pocket and pulled out another of the small bottles. It was at least his third, and pulling the cork with his teeth, he finished it off.

'Disgusting!' he spat, setting the bottle down on Kepler's desk. 'You start at the top and work down, room by room. If you see any more of those,' he glanced towards the bottle, 'bring them with you.'

Valerian looked at Willow, but she did not move.

'Valerian?' she asked.

'What is it?'

'Do I have to go upstairs by myself?'

'Yes. You'll be quicker than me. Don't tell me you're getting scared like Boy? Go. I'll be down here.'

He turned to the desk and began to open drawers and flip through books. She saw him look with interest at a piece of paper covered in writing and diagrams, which he folded roughly with one hand and put in his pocket. Then he went on rummaging.

Willow didn't understand how that would help find Kepler, and wondered who was really the more scared of what lay upstairs. But she turned and, with her heart in her mouth, set off for the first floor.

14

Willow thought about using the electrical light system, but it was frightening and probably dangerous. Seeing that Valerian was poring intently over papers at Kepler's desk, she lit the stub of the candle from the cemetery expedition with a match she found beside the fireplace.

She reached out a shaking hand to the handle of the first door she came to. Taking a deep breath, she turned the knob and pushed the door gently, and waited. Nothing. Holding the candle out in front of her she moved slowly into the room. There was no one there, nothing strange.

As she went through room after room and found nothing extraordinary in any of them, she began to calm down. Every one was as ordinary as could be imagined. This was just a normal house, the home of an educated man, with normal things in every room. Only the strange electrical switches on the wall showed that it was anything other than totally commonplace. She noted that the bed was made in what she assumed was the main bedroom, with clothes in neat piles on boxes, and everyday things sitting just where they should be.

There was no sign of violence, or robbery, or even untidiness anywhere.

Mystified, she went back to the study to find Valerian.

He was not there.

She swung around as if she were about to be attacked from behind at any moment.

When no one did, she risked calling out.

'Valerian! Valerian, where are you?'

She noticed a small door standing open in the far wall of the study. It was a secret door; she could see that it was made to look like part of the wooden panelling of the walls when it was shut.

Had it been open when they first came in? She crept across the room, trying not to make a sound.

Valerian, she thought angrily, *where are you?*

She made it to the small doorway and was not surprised to see a tiny flight of steps that turned immediately and led down, she presumed, to the cellar.

'Valerian!' she called.

Curse you, Valerian, she thought bitterly.

Still holding her lighted candle, she put her foot on the first step and began to descend. Two more steps and she noticed there was light coming from the cellar – more of that strange yellow electrical illumination.

She blew out her candle and went down.

At the bottom she stopped abruptly.

Valerian stood with his back to her, perfectly still, staring at the floor.

Around the walls were ranks of clay troughs, piled one on top of the other, so that there was almost no wall space left uncovered. In the top of each Willow could see metal plates, and from these came copper wires, which trailed crazily all around the stuff. There was a strong smell of some chemical. Willow supposed this was the source of the weird lighting in the house.

But Valerian was staring instead at the floor space in the centre of the cellar.

He turned and saw Willow.

'No?' he asked.

'There's no one,' said Willow, coming forward.

'Look at this,' said Valerian, nodding at the floor.

Willow stood by Valerian. It took her a moment to work out what she was looking at.

The floor of the cellar was made of packed earth, rammed as solid as brick. In its dusty surface someone, presumably Kepler, had dug a crazy pattern of trenches, each a few fingers wide and maybe a few deep. They criss-crossed and joined and snaked along and turned corners and struck out at odd angles, seemingly at random.

And they were filled with water. At least, Willow assumed it was water – it was hard to tell in the dim light. Whatever it was, it was liquid, a little murky from the packed soil channels through which it ran. For it was not still; somehow, it was moving.

Willow turned to ask Valerian something, but he anticipated her question.

'There's a small device at the far end, pushing it around. It is powered by the cells, just like the lights.'

But that posed another question.

'What . . . is it?' was the best way she could put it.

Valerian could not answer.

'I don't know. I haven't the slightest idea. I rather fear it means my friend has gone mad.'

Willow saw one more thing.

On the far wall, across the other side of the watery maze, was a blank space, not hidden by electrical paraphernalia.

Some words had been painted hastily on it with a thick brush. Willow recognised them as more Latin.

'What does that say?' she asked.

'The ramblings of a madman,' said Valerian sadly. ' "The miller sees not all the water that goes by his mill".'

Valerian stood staring at the nonsense on the floor and on the wall in front of them, and would say no more.

Willow sat down and put her head in her hands. She felt overwhelmed by despair. She had been carried into something she did not understand. It was easy to be swept along by Valerian when he was strong, but now he was weak and broken. He needed Willow, but she had no strength left. It was she who needed someone to guide her, and her only friend was running about the City miles away, on another crazy errand for his master.

They sat in the gloom of the cellar for a long time, until finally the clocks in the house began to chime midnight.

As the chimes died away one by one, Willow looked up at Valerian, who shook his head slowly.

'December the 28th is done,' he said.

December 29th

The Day of
Unnatural Developments

❦

They sat in the Tower, drinking tea and brandy and chewing on stale bread. All three were lost in their own thoughts, and the mood was grim.

It had been about two o'clock in the morning when Valerian and Willow got home. Boy, who had been back for hours, practically throttled Willow when he saw her. Hugging her hard, he hadn't let go of her until she made a small squeaking sound.

'How touching!' Valerian had said.

He looked terrible, and as far as Boy could tell, nothing had been done to his arm.

'Wasn't Kepler there?' Boy had asked.

Neither Willow nor Valerian replied, and that was answer enough.

'Did you succeed, Boy?' Valerian replied.

Boy's face fell. He stared at the floor.

'I'm sorry,' he said quietly.

'What?' spluttered Valerian.

'I couldn't even get past the door,' Boy protested.

'And you told them my name?' Valerian thundered.

'I said, I couldn't even get past the woman on the door.'

'Damnation!' shouted Valerian, and strode away across

the room, kicking over a pile of books, heedless of his damaged arm. He stood with his back to them, his shoulders rising and falling, staring at the floor. Finally he turned round, but he was no longer angry.

'Well, it was Childermas,' he said.

They looked at him blankly.

'The unluckiest day of the year.'

They thought about the graveyard, and the burial, and Valerian's arm and their fruitless trips across the City, and despite themselves, they all smiled.

'Fetch us food and drink,' Valerian had said, and Boy had found what he could, and taken it up to the other two in the Tower room.

When he got there he found Valerian and Willow standing by the table, above which was suspended the camera obscura.

Now, finally, Boy saw what it could do.

'Come and look at this,' whispered Willow.

Valerian turned to him.

'Haven't you seen this before?' he asked.

'No,' he said. 'You've never shown me what it does.'

Valerian shrugged.

'Come and see,' he said.

There were two parts to it. On the floor of the room stood a round table with a clear white circle set in its surface. Above it hung some large pieces of equipment, made up of wooden boxes and tubes of brass. So much Boy had seen before. But now he saw what it did. On the white surface of the table was an image of the City immediately outside the house. It was as if viewed from the very summit of the Tower, but slightly distorted; lines that should have been straight, like the sides of buildings, were gently curved, warped by the seeing-eye of the camera. But nevertheless it was an extraordinary image of the world outside, viewed from within.

And it was a moving image.

Boy watched, his mouth open, as they saw lights flickering in windows along the street, and smoke whispering out of chimneys and up into the night sky.

There was a long wooden lever that seemed to control the camera, and as Valerian moved it, the picture swung so that a different view from the roof of the house was shown on the table-top. They watched tiny figures scurry across it like ants.

'It's so . . .' said Boy.

'Isn't it,' said Valerian, nearly smiling. 'Unfortunately, despite its beauty, it illustrates the precarious nature of my current predicament.'

'What?' asked Boy, not really listening. He gazed at the moving picture in front of him, trying hard to tell himself it was real, that it truly was what was happening that very moment down in the streets beneath the Tower. Strangely, as Boy watched the ant-people hurry along, it gave him a sense of power.

'I had it built to see danger,' Valerian said. 'I keep watch here, night after night.'

Boy looked up. He could feel Valerian's fear. It was there between them, almost tangible.

'What for?' asked Boy. 'What are you watching *for*?'

Valerian spoke, and his voice was clear and calm and full of the promise of death.

'The end,' he said. 'Him. It. Whatever. Kepler said I was stupid to have this built. That it would do me no good even if I *did* see something coming for me. Maybe he was right, but at least this way I might get a little warning.'

Willow and Boy moved closer together and stared at Valerian, who turned his gaze back to the table. He moved the handle this way and that with his good arm, until he had scanned right around the Yellow House, checking all the streets and alleys.

Finally he pulled his eyes away.

'Did you find some food, Boy?' he asked.

They sat down to eat and the camera kept playing its dim but very real image of the outside world into the inner space of the Tower.

Valerian ate just a few mouthfuls and then fell silent, brooding in his great leather chair.

Boy looked at his master.

'You must eat,' said Willow, following Boy's gaze.

So should we, thought Boy. Valerian said nothing.

'How's your arm?' asked Boy. Then, getting no answer, 'You didn't tell me. What happened? Where's Dr Kepler?'

When Valerian still showed no sign of talking, Boy looked at Willow.

'Willow,' he said, 'where is he?'

'I – he–' began Willow, glancing at Valerian. 'It seems–'

'It seems!' cried Valerian. 'It appears! No! It *is* the case that Kepler has disappeared, and from the peculiar rantings in his cellar I think he has probably gone mad. My arm grows more painful, and I am running out of these.'

He waved a nearly empty phial at them.

'And then?' he barked, leaping to his feet. 'And then? Who knows! By the new year I shall be pieces of flesh strewn around this room!'

He stopped, aware that he was shouting. Boy and Willow stared at him, clinging to each other.

Boy felt panic slip up his back and squeeze his throat, making him want to be sick.

But Valerian had regained his composure and sat back down, as if resolved to his fate.

From his pocket he pulled another bottle of the drug. As he did so, both Boy and Willow saw a piece of paper fall from his pocket to the floor. It was the paper that Willow had seen Valerian take from Kepler's study.

Boy looked at Willow, her eyes wide with curiosity. Valerian took a long swig of his drug, then rinsed it down with a few mouthfuls of brandy. It was the weird hours of early morning, and as he slumped back in his seat he immediately fell fast asleep, snoring like an old, old man.

2

At dawn the camera played them a beautiful vision of the waking winter city, but they were all asleep, and the vision went unseen. Across the roofs and towers flooded a soft pink light that presaged snow, without doubt. Yet still it would not come and the City froze in its filth.

The Tower room had grown cold, and Willow lifted her head from the cushion on the floor. Her movement woke Boy. It was very early still, but they were soon wide awake. Boy felt awful. His arms were like wires, his legs like metal trunks, his neck like an iron bar. All he did was live, it seemed – live like one of Valerian's machines, with a heart-machine that pushed acid round his veins until they screamed in fear of what might be.

Boy had not slept well. Nightmares had ridden through his mind while he lay huddled on the floor. Unwanted thoughts returned to him again; those questions that Willow had been asking nagged at him. Who were his parents? Maybe it *was* important to know. Did he need to know, to know who he himself was? He was no longer sure.

He got up and walked around the room, stretching his legs. He found himself standing by the camera obscura table, staring at the moving image of the City waking up, coming to life.

136

Seeing that Valerian was still asleep, he dared to touch the handle that rotated the image. Willow came to stand by him and watched as Boy moved the lens around to view different scenes.

As he did so, a patch of light moved from the table and fell on the floor, illuminating the paper that Valerian had unknowingly dropped.

Boy looked at Willow, who picked up the paper. Her face creased.

'What is it?' asked Boy.

Willow shook her head.

'I don't know. Look.'

She held it for him to see.

Boy was not very good at reading, and the paper was covered in many symbols and signs that he knew were not words or letters at all.

But there was one word at the top of the paper that he could easily read.

BOY.

He shook his head, unable to understand what he was seeing, and then at last Valerian began to stir. Hurriedly Boy dropped the paper on to the table.

'We cannot stay here long,' Valerian said, rubbing his eyes with his good hand. That same hand began to search impatiently for another of the little bottles that took away his pain. 'The Watchmen will be looking for you. I have no doubt. Perhaps we should move to Kepler's house – it may be a little safer there . . .'

'But there was something,' said Boy.

'What?' said Willow.

'Why I couldn't get to see the Master of Burials.'

'Oh, spare us!' snorted Valerian. He crossed the room and began to fiddle with some bits of the camera, cursing occasionally when he couldn't manage with only one hand.

'I thought you might be interested,' Boy said to Valerian's back. 'What you said about him doing some strange studying and so on.'

Valerian ignored him.

'Tell me,' said Willow to Boy. 'What was it?'

'Well, I got talking to this woman at the gate. It seems he's obsessed with some animals he owns. It's all he spends his time doing. He's got this collection of animals, but they're all strange – he's got bird-headed snakes and dogs with cats' heads. There's cats with wings, and Willow, he's got dragons! They're tiny, but I saw them all!'

Willow stared at him in wonder.

'You're sure?' she said.

'I saw them with my own eyes. Snakes with birds' heads. Fish with a head at each end. And the dragons! But the thing is, they're all dead. I think he wants to make them live. I don't think he's doing his real job at all – he just spends all his time in this huge room under the glass dome, working on them.'

Willow shook her head.

'Dragons? Real dragons?'

'Yes,' said Boy. 'They're small, but–'

'Poppycock!' said Valerian. Neither of them had noticed that he had been listening. 'There are no such things.'

'But Valerian, I saw them!'

'Tell me,' Valerian said. 'What exactly did you see?'

Boy looked at Valerian and suddenly he hated him. Why did he have to treat him so badly all the time? Boy did his best, he always did what he was told, he worked hard, and yet all Valerian ever did was snipe and bark and criticise.

Valerian looked at him now, and Boy expected his face to be full of scorn, but as he held Valerian's gaze, he saw that Valerian was earnest, even interested. He was listening.

'What did you see?' asked Willow in a reassuring voice.

'Animals,' said Boy. 'And there were lots of them. And they were all weird. None of them looked like anything I've ever seen, or seen pictures of, or even heard of. They were all lying on his great table. On marble slabs.'

Boy paused. He pulled a face.

'Oh! There was so much blood.'

'Blood?' asked Valerian, with real interest.

Heartened, Boy went on.

'Yes, blood, and . . . things, from taking them apart.'

'The animals?' Valerian asked.

Boy nodded and scratched his nose.

'So he is dissecting them?' Valerian said.

'He's taking them apart,' said Boy. 'To see why they won't live, I suppose.'

'These animals,' said Valerian, 'all of them are strange, perverse things? Like nothing you have seen before?'

Boy nodded.

'And you think he's trying to make them live?'

Boy nodded.

'And he's taking them apart to see why they don't?'

Boy nodded.

Valerian shook his head.

'No,' he said gently, 'he's not taking them apart, he's trying to put them together.'

Boy thought. He thought for a long time, trying to remember exactly what he had seen.

'Could it be that?' Valerian asked.

Boy nodded.

'I think,' said Valerian, 'I think we should pay another

139

visit to the Master of Burials. We'll get the name of the cemetery where Gad Beebe is buried yet!'

He began to rummage all around the Tower room, pulling out various peculiar devices and equipment.

'But Valerian,' said Willow. 'Valerian!'

He kept on rummaging.

'Valerian!' she nearly shouted.

He paused.

'What is it?' he shouted back. 'We don't have the time! No time!'

'You were going to tell us. About what's happening to you.'

'Yes,' he snapped, 'but not now. I'll tell you on the way. Here, Boy, take this. It's delicate. Be careful! And Willow, this bag, if you please. Very good.'

Having checked around the outside of the building using the camera, they hurried from the Yellow House. As they went, Boy saw the paper with his name on it on the table and snatched it up, unseen. If Valerian didn't want it, then *he* did. It had his name on it after all – and Boy reasoned therefore that it belonged to him.

3

But Valerian did not tell them on the way. He did not tell them about the approaching horror, about the road which Fate was leading him down.

Instead he instructed them as they walked in the use of the pieces of apparatus they were carrying, repeating himself until they understood as much as they were able.

So now they stood inside the residence of the Master of City Burials. It was not easy to gain access to the Master of Burials, but Valerian had done it. He could be very persuasive.

Valerian had stared at the woman in the pillar, gazing deep into her eyes without saying anything for a long time. Finally he spoke, in a low and soft voice.

'You will go and tell the Master that Valerian is here to see him. Tell him I can make his animals live,' he said, and Boy and Willow watched amazed as without a word the old woman shuffled off her stool and went to do as she was bid. It was just as if Valerian had cast a spell on her.

Five minutes later a small door within the main door opened, and they hurried inside.

They stood facing each other in the grand entrance hall, sizing each other up. The Master was a short man, only a little taller than Boy. He was not quite as ugly as Green, but it still made Boy uncomfortable to look at him. His nose was pushed back, his eyes were small and overshadowed by huge hairy eyebrows. His hair was thin and greasy. He smelt terrible, his clothes were stained and despite their original quality were now little better than rags.

'Valerian! How strange to see you again.'

'A pleasure to renew your acquaintance. How long has it been?'

'Never mind that,' the Master snapped, his eyes, his brow creasing. 'How do you know of my work?'

'All the City knows of your work,' lied Valerian smoothly.

Good start, thought Boy, but the Master said nothing.

'I myself have admired your noble and valuable . . . investigations into this . . . subject,' Valerian went on.

He's losing it, Boy thought. *He doesn't really know what to say.*

'And I believe', Valerian concluded, 'that I may be able to help you.'

'Do what?' said the Master of Burials.

Valerian opened his mouth as if to speak, then shut it again.

'You said you could make them live,' said the Master of Burials.

This was the promise Valerian had made at the door. He shifted a little where he stood.

'Yes,' Valerian said. 'Yes, I believe I can.'

'Believe?' shouted the Master of Burials, furiously striding right up to Valerian. Though Valerian towered a foot or so above his head, Boy was amazed to see that the Master of Burials seemed to intimidate him. Boy had never seen anyone do this.

Fascinated yet nervous, Boy watched the struggle between them.

'Believe?' cried the Master again. 'I thought you said you *could* do it! If you can't you can get out of here and stop wasting my time. This is important work. Important! I have history to think of! How will my name be written across the pages of history if I cannot achieve this . . . masterpiece?'

The Master of Burials stared up at Valerian's face, then turned and spat on the floor.

'Get out of here!' he cried. 'Be away from here!'

Valerian stepped forward.

'No!' he cried. 'No, I can do it. With my two assistants here, I shall do it. Show me your animals. In return all I want is a little of your knowledge.'

The Master of Burials spun back to Valerian and held his gaze steadily for a long time.

'You had better be serious', he growled, 'or you will visit one of my cemeteries very much sooner than you had planned.'

He beckoned them forward, opening the door to the Dome.

'I already have,' said Valerian under his breath, and looked at Boy and Willow. 'Pray we get this right.'

4

Boy looked up to the roof of the Dome, where a few hours
before he had clung to the frosty glass like a human fly.

Boy and Willow, who had spent all of their fragile lives in
the City, were used to disgusting sights and noxious smells,
but nothing could have prepared them for this. Even
Valerian put his hand to his mouth and nose.

The inside of the Dome was the most ornate, the richest,
most extravagantly decorated slaughterhouse. Under the
glass dome above their heads the whole room was one vast
experiment. Solid wooden workbenches of elaborate design
formed a semi-circle. The top of each was finished with a
thick marble surface. There the horror began.

Animals, normal ones, lay dead all over the room. Larger
beasts rotted in boxes on the floor, while the smaller speci-
mens hung from hooks or lay in trays on the worktops. From
the darkest corners whimpers and howls came from various
unknown creatures.

Bits of bodies were lined up on other workbenches. A pair of
dogs' legs, a row of crows' wings and four cats' heads were just
some of the foul sights they took in with their hasty glances.

The Master was at the far side of the room, at the workbench where Boy had observed him through the glass late
the previous evening.

'Come on then,' he snarled. 'Come and see my beautiful creations!'

He waved them forward.

Boy and Willow stared at each other as they walked behind Valerian to the Master. They tried not to look at the pieces of animals around them, but they were fascinated and repelled in equal measure by what they saw. They were used to seeing carcasses and hunks of animals hanging in butchers' shops, but this minute and precise dissection of dogs, sheep, cats, birds – all still furred and feathered – was something else. Seeing this display of muscle, brain and bone made Boy wonder why things lived and then died, and what the difference was.

Then it got worse.

Boy and Willow caught up with Valerian, where he stood inspecting the Master's life's work.

'This is what I saw!' Boy whispered to Willow, but Willow had covered her mouth with her hand, whether to stifle a cry or to stop herself vomiting Boy couldn't tell.

On the ranks of marble slabs in front of them lay the animals. In a glass tray lay a creature the size of a cat. Its body seemed to be that of a weasel, but it had a long cat's tail and its head had once belonged to a large bird. There was no sign of any joins; the Master had evidently become a good craftsman in his time.

Next to the bird-weasel, in a tank of some foul chemical, a large fish with the head of a dog floated obscenely on its side. Further along the workbench Boy saw some of the dogs with cats' heads he had seen from outside, and the bird-headed cats.

And then there were the dragons. At first sight there seemed nothing else they could be but dragons – baby dragons. The largest was perhaps a foot long. It had a body of some greenish-grey lizard and seemed to have its own tail, and possibly even head, but then there were the wings: large, powerful, beautiful wings with feathers the colour of a golden sunrise adorned the creature's back.

As they looked closer they could just see a hint of some fine gut thread hanging down across the dragon's belly from where the wings were attached.

Valerian was hard at work now, letting his charm loose on the Master's ego. Valerian reasoned that anyone with an obsession like this had not only to be a little mad, but very self-centred too. He praised the Master's genius, his insight and his skill.

'And I curse the evil luck that has dogged you,' he went on.

'You are right!' cried the Master, his eyes glowing. 'It is bad luck. What else can have prevented every single one of my fine creations from living?'

'Indeed,' said Valerian.

'I do not merely throw these bodies together,' the Master went on. 'Oh no! Look!'

He took them to another table where he had some work in progress.

He lifted the skin over the haunches of a small deer and showed where he was attaching an eagle's legs.

'See? I attach every muscle to its partner, I link all tendons and tissues and fibres just as they should be. Every organ and vein and artery is thought of! I put back all the blood they lose. Why should they not live?'

'Why indeed?' echoed Valerian.

Boy and Willow looked at each other.

'None of them are sick', the Master rambled on, 'before they come here. They are all well. No disease nor even injury. I only allow the healthiest animals to go under my knife. Why then should they not live?'

'Indeed,' Valerian went on. 'Unless . . .'

He paused for effect, and the Master took the bait.

'What?' he cried breathlessly.

'Unless . . . I have some small knowledge in Natural Philosophies. It may be the case – it may be that there is some small but vital spark that is required to set life in motion.'

'And what is this vital spark?'

Valerian's on stage again, Boy thought. Acting a role, performing his magical skills, as he had done on the stage of the Great Theatre every night for years.

And now the Master was snared. Valerian turned to Boy and Willow with a flourish.

'The apparatus!' he declared, and Boy and Willow set their canvas sacks on the floor, carefully lifting out the things Valerian had given them to carry.

The Master stared at what he saw. He was a near wreck now, a mixture of excitement, worry and ignorance. Under Valerian's direction Boy and Willow set up the equipment.

From inside a wooden case Boy pulled a long glass tube, about two fingers thick and an arm's length. It had a metal cap at each of its ends and a small screw point for attaching a copper wire.

Willow lifted out her piece. It was a wooden and metal cased object, the size of a bucket. It was round, like a small barrel, with a handle on one of its flat sides. On its top was another screw point, to which Valerian quickly attached a length of copper wire. The other end was soon fixed to Boy's glass tube.

'Now,' said Valerian, 'which specimen do you want to live first?'

The Master was nearly beside himself with anticipation, hopping from one foot to the other.

147

'Now?' he cried. 'You can do it now? Just like that?'

'I can,' stated Valerian in a booming voice, 'on one con-
dition.'

The Master didn't even break step.

'Yes! Anything! Anything! Just make my animals live!'

'We require information. On a burial in the City. You
will promise us this if – when I make your beasts come
alive?'

'Yes,' said the Master, now almost weeping with excitement. 'I promise! You have my word!'

'Very well. Show us your latest creation. Is there anything
you have recently finished?'

'The dragon! The dragon!' shouted the Master, hopping
and pointing frantically.

Boy nearly blew it.

They lifted the equipment closer to the dragon, so that it
was within touching distance.

What if we really do bring it to life? thought Boy. *What if we
don't?*

But then Valerian was speaking.

'Now!' he said. 'Like I told you.'

Suddenly he winced in pain. He took another swig from
his small bottle, and after a few seconds lowered his head.
He nodded for them to start.

Willow knelt down by the barrel-thing, and began to wind
the handle. No one spoke. The tension in the room was truly
electric. The barrel hissed and crackled and fizzed.

Then Boy, who was holding the glass tube, made a mistake.

Hold it by the glass only, Valerian had warned, but Boy
forgot. Losing his grip on the tube and fearful of dropping it,
he touched one of its metal ends.

Instantly he shrieked. His hair stuck up in the air and his feet smoked slightly. He dropped the tube.

By a miracle it did not break.

'What is this nonsense?' screamed the Master. 'Are you trying to ridicule me?'

Valerian hurried forward.

'No, my friend! No! This is just a demonstration of the immense power we will instil in your creation!'

He picked up the tube and shoved it back in Boy's hands.

'Get it right, idiot!' whispered Valerian in his ear. 'Or I'll cut you up like one of these brutes!'

Dumbly Boy held the tube again. To be honest, he had little idea of anything for a moment or two. He felt as if his brain had been fried. His hair still stuck up vertically; he looked like a brush on legs. It felt like – it felt like the time he'd tried to pick the lock on the Yellow House and had been blown backwards across the street.

Boy realised that Valerian was using the same power now – something shown to him by Kepler, no doubt.

'Again!' cried Valerian. 'Willow. If you please.'

Willow wound again, and this time Boy held the tube only by the glass.

After a minute Valerian cried, 'Enough!'

He took the tube from Boy.

'Boy! The wires!' he cried.

Boy undid the wire from the tube, being very careful only to touch its leather sheath, avoiding the metal clips.

Valerian took one last look at the Master and approached the dragon.

'Behold!' he said melodramatically, and he touched the metal tip of the tube to the legs of the creature.

Immediately they began to twitch and flex.

149

Next Valerian touched the wings, and they too sprang into life, opening and then relaxing.

'It lives!' cried the Master. 'It lives! You have done it!'

He began to jump up and down on the spot, hitting his hands against the side of his head.

'I have done it at last! I am a genius!'

He approached Valerian, arms open wide. Valerian took a step backwards and held up his hand.

'Your promise,' he said.

The Master smiled.

'Anything you want! Just name it!'

'I need to know where someone is buried.'

'You have a name?' asked the Master, scuttling to the side of the room. There he pulled on a purple rope that hung from the ceiling. A distant bell tinkled and one of the Master's servants appeared. He looked a little surprised to have been called at all, and even more surprised to see that his master had guests.

'Sir?' enquired the servant.

'Get this man whatever he asks. You will need the alphabetical register of burials. Now leave me! I have many more animals to bring to life!'

Valerian looked nervously at Boy and Willow, who were looking at the dragon.

'Yes,' he said to the Master, 'I am sure you have much to do. We will leave you. All you have to do is turn the handle to charge the wand, then touch it to your animals. You may keep the equipment,' he added graciously.

Boy looked at the dragon. It had stopped twitching and now lay totally lifeless on the marble slab, but the Master of City Burials had not noticed. He was too busy winding the handle of the charger, talking to himself, trying to decide which of his bizarre beasts he would bring to life next.

Valerian looked at the servant.

'Would you mind?' he asked, and the servant led them away into a library stuffed with books full of the names of dead people.

Within two minutes the answer was in their grasp, but it was not one Valerian had expected.

There, in the register of dead people whose last names began with B, was a simple and clear entry.

Beebe, Gad. The Churchyard of Our Lady of Sorrows, Linden.

'Linden?' Valerian asked the servant. 'I've never heard of that part of the City.'

'That's because it's not in the City,' he said. 'It's a village.'

'Outside?' said Valerian. 'Outside the City?'

'Outside?' Boy echoed, unable to understand. 'We have to go outside?'

5

It was still only ten o'clock in the morning, even though they had already brought fantastical dead beasts to life, and found the key to Gad Beebe's whereabouts, and felt they had done more than a lifetime's work.

But they had hardly begun the struggles they would face before December 29th was over.

It was a fiercely cold morning. They stood outside the residence of the Master of City Burials, shivering in their boots. People hurried by, wrapped up against the biting cold in furs and capes.

'What do we do?' asked Boy.

'First', said Valerian, 'we get away from here. It won't be long before that madman realises his beasts will only twitch for a bit, and then we'll be in trouble. As if it weren't enough to have the Watch after us already.'

Willow and Boy had nearly forgotten about that. Nearly, but not quite.

'You mean you didn't really bring them to life?' asked Willow.

Valerian snorted.

'Of course not! No one could do that. It's just a trick that one of Kepler's teachers discovered some years ago.

Amusing but pointless. However, as I planned, it fooled him long enough to get what we were after.'

That was a pretty big gamble, thought Boy, but he said nothing.

'And now', Valerian went on, 'we have to get to the village of Linden. And quickly. We must find a coaching inn.'

'I know one!' said Willow. 'I was sent to meet Madame at the Black Four when she arrived in the City. We can find a coach there.'

'Good,' said Valerian. 'Lead on. I need the book.'

6

The Black Four was a handsome place, one of the best-looking inns that Boy had ever seen. He wished he'd known about it in his days on the streets, because it was filled with rich travellers coming and going, forgetting where they'd left their bags and valuables. It would have made easy pickings.

To the side of the tavern was a huge pair of double gates that swung open whenever a coach came or went. Just as they arrived, a vast black coach pulled by four black horses swung down the road and into the courtyard behind the inn.

'Look!' said Willow to Boy, tugging his sleeve. 'Just like the sign!'

She pointed at the sign of the Black Four, with a picture of a coach and horses just like the one that had arrived.

'Do you know anyone here?' Valerian asked Willow.

'I spoke to the landlord while Madame rested. She was tired after her journey.'

'Poor thing,' said Valerian unpleasantly. 'Well, what's his name?'

'Budge. Or Bridge, or something like that,' Willow said.

Valerian muttered impatiently and strode in through the doors of the inn, his long black coat swirling behind him. He made an even more alarming sight than usual. Tall, dressed

154

in black, with his grey-white hair straggling around his shoulders, he was usually quite imposing. Now, with his arm broken, hitched up and hidden under his soiled and muddied coat, and with eyes that burned despite having not slept properly for many nights, he looked like a minor demon.

Silence fell as he walked into the saloon bar of the inn. The room was filled with guests and servants. All eyes fell on Valerian and the two urchins who shuffled nervously behind him.

Valerian stopped in the centre of the room.

'The landlord?' he asked, fixing the serving girl nearest to him with his best glare.

Speechless, she nodded at the frosted glass door in the corner, too intimidated even to speak.

Valerian walked over to the door.

'Wait here,' he said to Boy and Willow, then strode in, unannounced.

Boy and Willow stood and waited. Gradually the people in the bar stopped staring at them and went back to their own business.

'What do you think this book is?' asked Willow.

'What?' asked Boy stupidly. Why did she always have to ask questions? By now all he wanted to do was sleep. They had been chasing around for almost three days, with little in the way of food and sleep. He just wanted to collapse in some small dark space and be left alone.

'The book,' said Willow impatiently. 'How is it going to save him?'

'Oh,' said Boy. 'I have no idea. But if Valerian thinks it will work, it probably will.'

'What's going to happen to him anyway on New Year's Eve?'

Boy shrugged.

'Ask him,' he said.

'I will. I just thought you might have some idea.'

'I'm hungry,' said Boy, changing the subject. 'Let's see if we can get Valerian to buy us something to eat.'

Willow agreed, and they pushed timidly through the door they had seen Valerian enter.

They found Valerian and the landlord shaking hands.

'Ah, children,' Valerian said, as if he was some kindly uncle. 'It is time to go. I have agreed a price for some transport to take us to Linden immediately.'

The landlord was smiling from ear to ear.

'Perhaps not my best coach, but since you are in a hurry you will not mind . . . ?'

Valerian nodded.

'Valerian,' said Boy, 'can we get something to eat?'

'Indeed,' said Valerian. 'Mr Birch here has packed a luncheon aboard our vehicle. Now we must be going. There is no time to waste. You have your money, do you not?' he added, turning to the landlord.

'Yes indeed, a very fair price,' he said. 'Well, this way then.'

Birch took them through a back door from his office and into the courtyard. The large sumptuous black coach they had seen arriving earlier was being made ready to depart.

'Our coach?' enquired Valerian amiably.

The landlord hesitated.

'Er . . . no,' he said. 'Yours lies just beyond.'

Without another word he hurried away. The large black coach pulled forward slightly, revealing their own transport. It was a joke. It was little better than a hay-wagon, a small cart that would have been better taking carrots from the fields to the markets. It was open to the skies and there was barely room in the back for the three of them.

The cart was hitched to a solitary and very old-looking horse, with a grey coat and a saddle-bag. Inside, their luncheon was a loaf and a bag of carrots, most probably for the horse. Holding the reins was an equally decrepit coach-man.

He stared at them, sucking his gums.

'The crook!' cried Valerian. 'This will not do! Where's he gone?'

'What's the use?' said the cart-driver. 'I'll get you there. You won't find anyone else to go out into the country today. It's going to snow.'

Valerian drew in his breath as if he might explode.

'Come on,' he said to Willow and Boy grimly.

They clambered aboard.

'Drive on!' Valerian shouted to the coachman, who jolted the beast into life.

They trotted, at a fair speed, out of the gates and on to the street. As they did so, the grand coach they had seen pulled out of the yard behind them. Valerian leant forward, with some difficulty because of his arm, to speak to the driver.

'That was where you met Madame?' Boy asked, nodding at the Inn.

Willow turned to Boy, smiling.

'That's funny. I was just thinking about her too.'

'You could still go back to her,' said Boy quietly to Willow. 'All you have to do is jump off. Go back to the theatre. She'd take you back.'

Willow turned to look at Boy.

'No,' she said sadly. 'I hated her. She hated me. I'm sick of it. And anyway, she'd probably turn me over to the Watch for Korp's murder.'

'I can't believe you think working for Valerian is any better,' said Boy.

'I don't. I mean, I'm not working for Valerian.'

'Then what are you doing here?' asked Boy.

'Don't you know?' She said no more.

'What, Willow?' asked Boy. 'I don't understand.'

'I thought you could have guessed. You should know. You were alone for so long. All those years on the street, that you can't even properly remember now. And then you found Valerian, or rather he found you.'

She glanced up to check that Valerian was still busy in discussion with the coachman about their route.

'And he's awful,' she whispered. 'He beats you, he ignores you, he's unpleasant and ungrateful and foul. And yet you stay with him. Why?'

'Because I . . .' said Boy. 'Because I want to be with someone.'

'Exactly,' said Willow, and looked over the side of the cart at the buildings going by. 'I want to be with you,' she said, but not loud enough for Boy to hear.

They rode towards the City wall.

Valerian struggled to sit back down, having got little joy from the driver over their journey and its destination. Boy lent a hand to Valerian and helped him sit back down.

Valerian grunted with pain.

'Gods! It's cold this morning,' he muttered.

'Look, here are some blankets,' said Willow, rummaging under the side benches that were supposed to provide seating. She pulled out two large, moth-eaten blankets, and they were grateful for them.

Willow spread one over Valerian and tucked it under him.

'Thank you, Willow,' he said, and shut his eyes as they bounced on through the City.

Willow and Boy spread the other blanket around them as best they could. They chewed slowly on the bread and carrots, grateful at least for some food, but Boy's mind was on other things. The cart was too exposed. Anyone could look at them, and at any moment he expected to see a gang of red- or pink-plumed Watchmen come charging down the street after them. But none did. They were just another small cart with some human cargo winding its way through the City, a scene that was occurring a thousand times in every corner of the vast metropolis. No one paid them the slightest attention. No one could tell that the three figures in the back of this particular cart were engaged in a most unusual and deadly history.

7

It took the rest of the morning for the cart to get to the City gates. It was painfully cold now, and as they huddled in the back of the cart under the blankets and passed under the massive arch of the South Gate, the first few feeble flakes of snow fell, just as the driver had predicted.

The South Gate was a vast stone construction. Its entire surface was covered with bizarre stone carvings, designed by the City Architects to impart improving lessons to the populace. It seemed that much of the populace was even now gathered in and around the South Gate, a busy market place. No one paid the instructional carvings any attention as they called and shouted to each other in the process of trading. Around them the City walls were still decorated with fir tree branches and other greenery from the festivities of a few days before.

A few days, thought Boy, *but it feels like months*. The dead days had a knack of stretching themselves. When the days are out of the normal flow of time, time can stand very still indeed. All time, and no time. The dead time of the dead days.

Their cart approached the gates, for a heartbeat they were under the flying stone arch, and then they were outside.

'Have you ever been out of the City, Valerian?' asked Boy.

'Oh yes,' he said. 'Many times, though not for many years. The last time – I suppose the last time was fifteen years ago.'

'And you've never been outside since?' asked Willow.

Valerian didn't answer, lost in his memory. Then he seemed to hear Willow and shook his head.

'That was enough for a lifetime,' he said grimly. 'For a lifetime.'

'What's it like?' asked Boy.

'You'll see,' said Valerian, indicating the changing landscape around them.

Boy and Willow had never believed there could be so little of everything. So much empty space.

The last few miles through the City had been much like any other, but there had been a subtle change. The outermost parts were the poorest and the houses the most dilapidated. The coachman had picked up the pace a bit as they wound through some particularly unpleasant areas, even though it was midday.

Now there was nothing. Around them lay mile upon mile of empty fields. Away in the distance were forests and beyond them some hills. Boy and Willow were scared by it, feeling exposed and vulnerable.

The snow was falling thickly. For days it had threatened but had held off. It was as if the promise of all that snow had been stored up for this moment, for very soon the world had disappeared under a blanket of pure whiteness.

Into Willow's mind once more came a picture of herself, as a little girl, playing in the snow somewhere in the countryside. It seemed more real this time. She was with her parents, and she had the feeling they had been going to see someone. But no more would come, and the vision evaporated.

*

'Where is this place?' asked Boy. 'Linden?'

'You are becoming too much like the girl,' said Valerian irritably. 'Too many questions.' He took a swig from his bottle.

But when Willow asked the same question, he relented.

'It may take some hours to get there.'

'Have you been there before?'

'No.'

'Valerian.'

Valerian stowed the bottle back in his coat pocket with some difficult, and looked up at Willow.

'What is it, girl?'

'What's happening to you? What's going to happen?'

Valerian stared out at the whitening world around them.

'You said you were going to tell us.'

The cart trundled on. Its driver did not look back once. The snow fell ever harder as they made their way to a minor track which plunged them into dense forests of silver birch. The trees were stripped of their leaves and had a ghastly air of desolation about them. The wheels of the cart slipped against the mud of the track, frozen hard into great ruts. All around them was the absolute silence of the dormant forest.

And as the old nag led them ever closer to the grave of Gad Beebe in the remote village of Linden, Valerian spoke.

'You remember I said that I had last ventured out of the City fifteen years ago. I will tell you about that excursion.

'Then I was still a young man. Perhaps. But I could feel time was passing for me. Passing too quickly. I had left the Academy. I was not well-liked at that time. In fact I was disgraced. In my defence I can only say that I was doing what

162

my timid colleagues were too scared to do! If you understand.'

Boy shook his head but said nothing to disturb Valerian. He had waited years to hear this story, and he wanted nothing to distract Valerian from its telling.

'How can I explain? I was a Natural Philosopher too, then. I studied every aspect of Natural Philosophy – what some younger men are now calling "Science". I studied hard. Like Kepler still . . . like Kepler. I studied all branches of investigation into our world. So did we all. Myself, Kepler, and those who later denounced me.

'The intense pursuit of any idea that takes complete possession of me is one of the qualities that makes me different – sometimes for good, sometimes, I dare say, for evil – from other men. It was because I had a greater thirst for knowledge, a greater hunger and desire to know all that could be known, that I became interested in stranger aspects of these studies. Dark, strange knowledge. Hidden knowledge.

'And I soon learnt that our modern thinking is but half the story. That there is a hidden world of a precious and powerful nature that has been known for as long as man has been thinking and doing.

'In my stupidity, in my pride, I rushed to share this with my colleagues, but I was a fool, for they shunned me. The things I did were dark and powerful, yes, and they were afraid of me. They threw me out! They turned their backs on me! And I was disgraced.

'In my anger, their treatment of me only served to make me delve even deeper into these unknown forces. I worked long and hard and began to create things I should not have done. I began to conjure powers that should not be known. I summoned them. Small spirits at first, then greater and greater life-forms, with the power to change the world if they so desired.

'I thought I could control them. And indeed I could. I summoned these things from their hidden places and they did my bidding. Small matters like money were no problem. That was easy in those days. They did whatever I wished. Now I would not dare . . .'

He paused for a moment.

There were so many questions Boy longed to ask, but still he did not want to break the spell. Willow, however, had the habit of asking questions, and so she did. It was a simple one.

'Why?' she said.

'There is something else,' said Valerian. 'Something else I have not told you – someone else, I should say. A woman.

'She was fair, like the clear moon that shone down on my labours night after night. She was beautiful. Her hair was long and blonde like golden corn, but she always wore black. The beauty of this extreme drove me to distraction.

'Yes, she was beautiful. But more than that. Light danced behind her eyes, such eyes as I have never seen before nor since. Her voice sparkled like a glittering stream, and her mind was both sharp and playful.

'She was rich. Her father was a great and powerful noble-man. She was unattainable. She would not even have noticed a nobody like me, thrown out even from my college. And so I resolved to make something of myself. To make myself powerful and rich and strong. Then she could be mine.

'And so, having learnt of a most powerful conjuration, I summoned a thing – a thing I should not have done. I thought it would help me, grant me my wishes. And so it did. But I was oblivious to the price for all the power and wealth I was granted.'

Valerian stopped again, wincing at a twinge of pain from his arm.

'Look at me now!' he said bitterly as he fished in his pocket for the bottle. It was nearly empty and he drained the last few drops and threw the bottle over the side of the cart to land unheard in the thick snow. 'A wreck! This cart may as well be taking my coffin to the ground as taking us to God-knows-where in this forsaken land.'

'Don't say that!' cried Boy.

'No?' asked Valerian bitterly. 'I have now a little over two days to live unless there's a way out of this mess. I have not yet told you of the price I was set. I was granted power and wealth and I got them. And there was her. I was granted the power to have her.

'In return, I gave my life. I did not realise it at first, but the conditions were spelt out. I was given fifteen years. Fifteen years to use my power and money and make what I could with it, and at the end of which I will belong to the thing I summoned. My life is his. My body and soul are his. It is over, then. And it was almost exactly fifteen years ago that I made this pact, this bargain, deep in the forest. On New Year's Eve.

'Do you think it's strange to risk so much?'

Neither Boy nor Willow answered.

'I was blind. Love had made me blind, and I thought a night – even an hour with her would be enough. And I was arrogant, and I knew that in fifteen years I would find a way out of the pact. How clever I was then! How stupid!

'At first I was still foolish enough to think I would find a way out, but as the years passed I grew older and wiser and doubt began to grow. I had spent all my money, and never again will I summon those powers to help me get more.'

165

Willow was about to ask Valerian the woman's name, but Boy asked a different question first.

'And Kepler's been helping you find a way out?'

Valerian nodded.

'So why didn't you ask him for help sooner? Why wait until the last few years to get his help?'

Valerian spoke to Boy, but his gaze went right through him.

'Kepler and I had fallen out at the time of my making the pact. We . . . disagreed over something. We did not see each other for maybe ten years. But many things can be forgiven in time, and when I went to see him again he agreed to help me find the book.'

'What did you disagree about?' Boy asked.

A shadow crossed Valerian's face. He chose to ignore this question, but some intuition told Willow it had something to do with the woman.

'My time is up,' he said instead. 'My only chance lies with the book. I had heard of it, and when I told Kepler about it he spent many months finding out about it. His knowledge of ancient libraries is second to none. He gathered references to the book – a mention here, half a line there – until we learnt that if it still existed, it was probably in our very own City. Then we began to believe we might actually find the thing itself.

'It is a book full of such ancient and powerful knowledge that we believe it contains some spell or other way of breaking the contract I am under. Indeed Kepler firmly believes that it contains the answer. From his researches he discovered that it is no normal book. For it is not just pages with writing, information to be learnt, the mundane and the extraordinary. No, it is more than that. Kepler believes that the book is itself a magical device, and each person who looks into it learns something different – something about only themselves, the thing uppermost in their mind, the thing they most want to know . . .

'For five years we have been tracking it down. About a year ago we thought we had it. We were mistaken. Then a few months ago it was promised to us, and again we were tricked. It is a powerful thing, and across the years many people have struggled to claim possession of it.

'I was relying on things happening more quickly than they have, but maybe there is still time. Maybe. Kepler was sure of it, and despite . . . the things that occurred between us, he is my one salvation in all this.'

Valerian broke off, obviously thinking of Kepler.

Willow watched him, her mind wandering to something Valerian had said.

'Valerian?' she asked, brushing more flakes of snow from her hair.

'What?' he asked, almost inaudibly.

'The woman. The woman you did it all for. What happened to her?'

Valerian lifted his head and his cold stare ran straight through Willow.

'She?' he said, 'She . . . rejected me. Despite the enchantment, somehow she still rejected me. I never saw her again.'

There was silence.

Willow still wanted to know her name, but could not bring herself to speak. Boy wondered how someone could risk so much, face such horrors, enter such a pact, all for someone who would cast them away, but Willow, looking at Boy, could feel differently.

To risk everything for someone – that was something she understood.

'Boy,' she said, quietly, 'I'm cold.'

'Come here,' he said, and put his arm around her.

8

Silence fell over them as the cart ploughed on through the snow-bound forest.

Boy felt a mixture of emotions, and none of them good — fear, horror, sadness, hopelessness. Willow felt pity, and a dread of Valerian's situation that she felt she could not begin to cope with.

And Valerian? Who knows what deep and dangerous thoughts ran through his disturbed mind?

Dead to everything around them, they plodded on through mile after mile of snow-laden silver birch forests. Dimly, it seemed to Boy impossible that there could be so many trees and impossible that it could snow for so long. And yet the trees went on for ever and so did the snow.

Willow, though smaller than Boy, kept a firm grip on the blanket spread across them despite the fact that she was virtually insensitive to everything around her. Boy had been lulled by the rhythmic stagger of the cart into a half-sleep, in which the waking world and his troubled imagination fought for control. And then his imagination won. He plunged into a bizarre sequence of mind-pictures in which he was back in his favourite kind of place: a small, confined darkness. Yet there was horror somewhere nearby, something that wanted to be bad to him. He scurried deeper into the cramped black spaces until he felt safer, only to feel the hunting presence coming closer and closer once more. In his perverse dream-world he could feel himself being pulled further away from himself, until at last there was an answer and he *became* the small dark space himself, and in doing so was free.

And Valerian?

There was nothing. He had either passed out or slept as they went on through the paper-white trees, and the soft, deathly snow.

And yet . . . and yet, then there came the end to the trees.

Dusk was only an hour or so away when they emerged from the forest at last. Far off in the distance stood a wretched little village.

The driver spat one word back over his shoulder.

'Linden!'

Then, in a cracked and bleak voice, he began to sing. It was a miserable song and suited all their moods as they were roused from their fitful sleep.

> *In the morning you should think*
> *You might not last unto the night,*
> *In the evening you should think*
> *You might not last unto the morn.*
> *So dance, my dears, dance,*
> *Before you take the dark flight down.*

As he finished his dirge, they pulled into Linden. It was just a handful of houses, an old watermill and the odd barn. For some reason, however, it had an imposing and ancient church that towered in the dusk like a man-made mountain of cut stone.

There, past a rickety fence, lay their goal – the church-yard.

The driver pulled the horse to a stop.

'We shouldn't need long,' Valerian said to him.

'I don't care how long you need,' said the driver. 'We can't go back tonight.'

He got down and started to unhitch the horse from the cart.

Valerian turned to argue, but the old man cut him off.

'If you don't get out of there before it's unhitched you'll fall off,' he grunted. 'And by the look of your arm I don't think you'd want that.'

Defeated, Valerian scrambled down, grimacing with pain as he reached the ground.

'Is it getting worse?' asked Willow.

'Do you have any left?' asked Boy, and Valerian pulled a final, somewhat larger bottle of Kepler's magic drug from his pocket.

'That's all,' he said forlornly. He turned to the driver who was leading his horse over to one of the barns.

'Where are we to stay then?'

The driver didn't look back as he called, 'You should have thought of that before you set out.'

He led the horse into the barn and followed him inside. The door closed. There was a time, Boy knew, not too long ago, when Valerian would have fought the driver, compelled him to do his bidding. But now Valerian was a different man from the one Boy had grown up serving. A broken man, he was nearly spent.

They looked around the village. Even in the fading light they could see it all from where they stood.

There were three houses, each standing by itself on a patch of land with a low wooden fence. Each had a variety of little shacks and outhouses clustered behind it, and vegetable gardens that ran down to where the fields proper started.

There was the water mill. It had a large mill pond up-stream, frozen solid and now covered in snow as well. The entire mill race seemed to be frozen, though water must have been moving underneath the icy surface. The wheel was frozen solid, and long fingers of icicles hung down from the blades that in summer would have ducked powerfully into the water.

There were two large barns, into one of which the coach driver had vanished with his horse. The other was a little smaller. And there was the church.

There was no one around, though they could see firelight inside some of the windows and could hear the sounds of a village preparing to rest at the end of a winter's day. A dog barked behind one of the houses. A rickety door slammed. They felt utterly alone.

'I don't like the countryside,' said Willow.

'Hmm,' said Valerian. 'It can be a little . . . quiet.'

'What are we going to do?' asked Boy. 'Where are we going to sleep?'

'We're not,' said Valerian. 'The first thing to do is find what we came here for – the book. Then we'll get a horse and take ourselves back.'

'You mean . . . steal one?' asked Willow.

'If we have to,' said Valerian. 'I'll be damned if I spend the night in this hole.'

He realised the other meaning of his words and fell silent.

9

It did not go well.

They made their way to the churchyard.

'We'll need to find a spade,' said Valerian. 'There'll be something in the mill . . .'

He tripped and fell forward, landing on his knees.

'Damn this arm!' he spat.

Willow and Boy knelt beside him.

'Don't fuss!' he snapped at them, and they jumped back.

He struggled to his feet, but this time when Boy and Willow each put a hand out to help him, he did not argue.

Supporting Valerian between them, they staggered to the churchyard, where they leant him against the wall on a low buttress that ran around the outside.

He shook his head.

'You'll have to do it,' he whispered. He drank the first of his last bottle and pulled a face. 'You two will have to do it.'

Boy and Willow looked at each other.

'Dammit!' cried Valerian. 'I can't move for pain. I can't walk and I certainly won't be able to dig. You'll have to do it.'

They nodded in unison.

'Boy! Go to the mill. They must have some sort of shovel for moving the corn. Girl! Start looking. Remember, Gad Beebe is the–'

'Of course I remember,' said Willow. 'I found the name for you!'

She glared at Valerian, who hung his head. He lifted his hand and waved them feebly away.

'Come on,' said Boy quietly.

The light was failing fast but there was just enough to see the names on the gravestones, though Willow had to scrape the snow off a few of them to be able to read the name of their occupants.

Before Boy returned with the spade, Willow had made a full circuit of all the stones in the small yard. The name Gad Beebe was not among them.

Boy found her standing in a far corner of the graveyard.

'Which one is it?' he asked, clutching a long-handled wooden spade.

She shook her head.

'He's got it wrong,' she said. 'It's none of them.'

Boy stared at her.

'I'm too afraid to tell him.'

'You must be wrong. Let's have another look.'

'Boy–'

'We can't tell him that,' said Boy. He looked over to the far side of the churchyard where Valerian leant slumped against the wall of the church. 'Let's have another look.'

So they did. Boy felt a strange sense come over him as they searched the stones. A sense of being outside himself, of not needing to be there in the snowy village deep in the countryside. Yes, he was cold and hungry and miserable, but it was something more than that. It felt as if he was in the wrong place, going the wrong way.

Maybe he was right, because though they searched the

graveyard carefully until the light was nearly gone, Gad Beebe's last resting place was not to be found.

When they got back to Valerian he looked like death. The snow had stopped but it was very, very cold. He looked old and on the point of freezing.

He lifted his head as they approached. His eyes read their faces and they were spared the job of having to tell him.

'He's not there, is he,' Valerian said, but it was not a question.

His head dropped.

Boy, still clutching the spade, opened his mouth.

'Don't say "What are we going to do?"' Valerian said without looking up, 'because I don't know.'

'We need to get inside somewhere,' said Willow.

Boy nodded.

'Valerian?' he said. 'Let get inside somewhere. Yes?'

Valerian didn't reply.

'What about here?' suggested Willow. She meant the church.

'Very well,' said Valerian hoarsely. 'Help me up.'

Gratefully, Boy and Willow pulled and levered Valerian into a standing position. It seemed that his legs had practically frozen solid where he leant against the church. Boy put the spade under his arm for him to use as a crutch, and they crept slowly forward.

Once again they staggered through the graveyard, taking the path to the church door. It was not locked and they pulled Valerian out of the bitter, biting wind.

The heavy oak door swung behind them, pulled shut by a counterweight. A massive church silence descended.

They settled Valerian on a pew at the side of the aisle. There were candles burning all around the altar and in other

174

alcoves. Having been lit for the festival, they would be kept alight for twelve days. Willow was mightily glad to see them.

'Come on,' she said to Boy, and started to collect them two at a time. They took about two dozen thick and tall goose-white candles back to where Valerian lay on the pew, and placed them on the flagstones in front of him. The effect of the flames from the tallow candles was impressive, like a small fire, and slowly Valerian came back to life.

Using the spade as a prop he pushed himself upright, until he was sitting more or less vertically on the pew.

'Well,' he said, 'let me ask you a question, Boy. Willow. What are we going to do now?'

'Don't joke,' said Willow.

'I'm not,' said Valerian. 'Everything I have tried has failed. I have been foiled at every twist and turn. All my decisions have turned out badly and now we are sitting in a freezing church in the middle of nowhere with no way of getting home and even if we did . . . my prospects are not good. So I think that you may as well decide what we do next?'

What is there to do? thought Boy miserably.

'We ought to find something to eat,' he said. 'We could ask at one of the houses. The driver must be staying in one of them. Maybe he'll help us.'

'Him?' said Valerian. 'That swine!'

'Well,' said Willow, 'we can't just sit here.'

She looked at Valerian, who was staring into space behind her head.

'*Non omnem videt molitor aquam molam praeterfluentem!*' he said.

'Valerian!' Boy cried. 'Stop it! You're scaring me!'

But Valerian rose to his feet and pointed at the wall.

'*Non omnem videt molitor aquam molam praeterfluentem!*' he said again.

175

'Valerian!' Boy shouted. 'Stop it!'

'No! Look! *Non omnem videt molitor aquam molam praeter-fluentem.* "The miller sees not all the water that goes by his mill." Willow and I have seen that before!'

There on the wall behind them was a huge shield, a coat of arms, painted on to the stone. Its central image was a waterwheel, just like the sort frozen solid in the winter's night outside the churchyard. Emblazoned across the top was the motto Valerian had read.

'I don't understand,' said Boy. 'What's so important—'

'Look!' said Willow. 'There!'

She ran over and pointed to the name beneath the crest. William Beebe.

'Beebe! This is his family crest!' said Valerian. 'It must have been a wealthy family. He's not buried outside at all. He's in here somewhere! Look! There's another!'

He pointed.

A little further down was the same coat of arms, with another name. Daniel Hawthorn Beebe.

'Quick!' Valerian cried, his strength miraculously returning. 'Quick!'

But Boy was already scampering down the church.

Joseph and Sophia Beebe.

John Israel Beebe.

And then, there it was.

Gad Beebe.

'Here!' called Boy. 'It's here!'

Willow ran to him, Valerian not far behind.

'I can't believe it!' said Valerian. 'He really exists! Or he did exist, anyway. To see the name, written!'

'But where is he?' asked Boy. 'He can't be in the wall.'

Valerian turned and looked down at Boy, pulling one of his most devilish smiles. Then he raised a finger in front of boy's face and turned it slowly so it pointed straight at where Boy was standing.

'Indeed,' he said. 'He's under your feet.'

Boy shrieked and jumped back. By the light from Willow's candle they could see an inscribed stone in the floor.

'Fetch that spade, will you, Boy?' said Valerian. 'Let's get on with it.'

Boy brought the spade over.

'When was he – you know – put here?' he said.

'I have no idea,' said Valerian. 'Why?'

'Well, I was wondering what sort of – what we might find.'

'Ah! Well, let's have a look at the date.'

Valerian knelt down, wincing as he did so.

'Bring that candle a little closer, will you? Good. Now. There we are. Years ago, so no need to worry. It won't be too foul. Anyway, it's the book I'm after, not the man.'

Still Boy dithered.

'Get on with it,' said Valerian icily.

Boy shoved the tip of the spade along the crack between the stone with Beebe's inscription and its neighbour. He levered it back and pulled. He went flying backwards as the spade splintered on the stone, which had not moved.

Boy picked himself up.

'Are you all right?' Willow asked.

'Never mind him,' said Valerian. 'We'll have to find something else to prise it up. Quick. Someone could come at any time.'

They found a tall, heavy candlestick, its massive spike exposed when Willow removed one of the candles.

Putting the metal spike into the crevice, Boy and Willow both leant on it with all their weight. There wasn't as much leverage as with the spade, but the candlestick was strong and with a sudden lurch the slab lifted an inch or two.

177

'Quick!' said Valerian. 'Get something under there!'

With his foot Boy slid the handle of the spade under the stone flag.

Still cold, and not having eaten all day, everything they did now exhausted them. They rested for a moment, panting after the exertion.

'What are you waiting for?' Valerian growled. 'Get on with it!'

Wearily, they lifted the candlestick and shoved the top end as far as it would go under the small space they'd created.

Again they pushed down and the slab lifted some more.

'Lean to the side,' ordered Valerian, and they did. The slab rolled along the top of the candlestick and away from the hole. Repeating this motion a couple more times freed the stone completely.

'Now dig,' said Valerian, pointing at the patch of earth they had exposed.

Boy picked up the broken spade. Most of its face was still usable and he began to lift out the earth.

It came away surprisingly easily, and before even a few minutes had passed the spade hit the top of something else wooden.

Valerian could hardly contain his frustration. He hovered by the hole, grunting and cursing as Boy and Willow pulled at the dirt with their bare hands.

'Why do we always end up doing this?' muttered Willow as she and Boy once again scraped in grave-soil.

'Shut up and dig,' said Boy.

And then it was done. They had exposed the surface of the coffin.

'Oh no!' said Boy. 'Not again!'

'What is it?' asked Valerian, his voice tense.

Boy shook his head.

'The box is broken.'

He leant down and with one hand was able to pull up the top section of coffin lid. Just like the one in which Valerian had nearly met his end, the top third of the lid had been broken, snapped off to leave a jagged edge of flimsy wood.

Boy threw the wood to one side. He looked back into the hole. Willow gasped. Inside lay a skeleton, mostly clean but only mostly.

Its arms were folded across the tatters and rags of its chest.

And that was all. There was no book.

'It can't be!' cried Valerian. 'Look further in! At the feet!'

Boy didn't move. He looked down at the skeleton and knew he could not make himself get that close to it.

'Do it!' shouted Valerian.

'I . . .' Boy stammered, 'I can't.'

Valerian stopped and then kicked the candlestick hard so it skittered away into some pews.

'I'll do it,' said Willow hurriedly, and before Valerian could say another word, she held up a candle and peered into the depths of the grave.

She stood up.

'Nothing,' she said.

'Tricked!' Valerian said bitterly.

'Then . . . ?' began Boy.

'Yes,' said Valerian. 'Yes. This looks rather like a dead end.'

10

'Can't you just run away somewhere?' asked Boy. 'Hide? Until after New Year?'

'If only it were that simple,' said Valerian, 'I would already be on the other side of the world. The force with which I made my pact . . . is powerful. It transcends time and space. It will come for me wherever I am on New Year's Eve. The day after tomorrow.'

They were sitting in the church, by the candles, trying to keep warm.

'But there is something,' said Valerian suddenly. 'How could I have forgotten . . . the motto? The Beebe family motto! Willow, I said we have we seen it before! Where?'

'At Kepler's house. In the basement. But why?'

Valerian stood up.

'Why?' he said slowly. 'Because Kepler must have known about Gad Beebe. He knew about his family motto. Perhaps he already has the book! Come!'

'What?' cried Boy. 'Where?'

'Back to the City. To find Kepler. We must find him! He knows something. Find him and we may find the book.'

'Do you think he was here?'

'No. No, I don't think so, but he knew about Gad Beebe. Now we just have to work out where he's gone.'

'But how will we get back?' asked Willow.

As she spoke the clock in the tower of the church above them began to strike midnight.

'Willow,' said Valerian, 'it's time to steal a horse.'

December 30th

The Day of
Unfailing Coincidence

❧

1

But things were not to turn out that way.

'No!' Willow had said for the fourth time, and Boy had worried about what Valerian might do to her.

'No,' she said. 'You can't just take someone else's horse!'

But Valerian did nothing to her. It almost seemed he was soft with Willow. Boy watched, amazed, as she argued in the persistent snowfall outside the villager's stable.

'I have no money left!' shouted Valerian. 'We must get back to the City and there is no other way.'

Finally Boy at least managed to get them to have their argument inside. In the stable they saw why they had found no trace of the driver – his cart had gone and so had the beast.

But they could make out the shapes and smell of two young horses.

'These people have nothing!' cried Willow. 'You can't take their horses from them!'

'And if I don't, I'll be dead,' Valerian said, but it seemed there was less strength in his words than there might have been. Boy wondered if his arm was affecting him. At times he seemed delirious with pain.

'That's not their concern, is it?' Willow said.

'No,' said Valerian, sounding exhausted. 'No, it's mine.'

He stared into Willow's eyes and there was a stand-off. Boy held his breath, and in the silence of the snowstorm they heard an angry cry.

It came from the direction of the church.

Boy stuck his head through the door and just as quickly pulled it back in.

'They've found our mess!' he hissed. 'In the church! There's at least three of them and they're coming this way!'

Valerian looked at Willow.

'When this is all over I'll come back and buy them a dozen horses,' he said. 'I promise!'

Willow said nothing.

Boy ran over to her.

'Willow! Come on!'

It would never even have occurred to Boy that it might be wrong to steal the horses. In the way he'd grown up, first on his own and then with Valerian, he'd learned different lessons. If you needed something, and you could get it without getting caught, you took it. Willow thought differently, and he could tell she was very serious about it.

'Willow!' he cried again.

'All right!' she said at last. 'Do it! But you have to promise! A dozen horses!' she added to Valerian.

'Yes, yes,' he said. 'Come on!'

It was too late.

Boy pulled the stable door open to find a group of four or five villagers.

They were large men, and their burning torches and sharp-edged farming tools looked ghastly in the darkness and the swirling snow.

Boy backed into the barn, trying to think fast but failing.

'Come on!' Valerian called.

He spurred his horse forward, but when the animal came close to its masters it stopped. One of the villagers put his hand up to the horse's cheek and whispered to it. Immediately the horse rose on its back legs and let out a loud whinny. Valerian slipped from the horse's back and fell into the thin straw on the stable floor.

As he hit the ground he howled with pain and then blacked out.

Two men stepped forward, and Boy saw the cart driver behind them. Boy swore at himself, and at Valerian, for having been so stupid as to trust him not to have said anything about their arrival in the village. Another of the villagers lowered an old but sturdy pitchfork at Boy, pointing its three prongs at his throat. The man was not tall, but strong and broad. His face was weather-worn and dirty. He was angry.

'Now,' he said, 'my fine City boy, what have you done to our church?'

'Us?' said Boy.

The villager swung the pitchfork, hitting Boy across the side of the head with the handle. Willow rushed as he fell next to Valerian.

'No so fast!' shouted one, but Willow took no notice. She crouched by Boy. He did not move.

'You've killed him!' she screamed.

The man spat in the straw.

'Not yet,' he said. 'He's breathing yet.'

With relief Willow saw it was true. She looked about her. Boy and Valerian both lay, out cold, in the foul-smelling straw of a barn in a village miles away from the City. Around her stood a gang bent on revenge, and she knew there was nothing she could do.

2

Dawn rose on the morning of December the 30th, but Boy and Willow did not see the day break. Valerian did not see anything.

Boy had come round from the blow to his head quite soon, and immediately been sick in the straw. He put his hand to his head, and felt blood and broken skin. He had a murderous headache.

The villagers had taken Willow and Boy back to the church, and had carried Valerian none too gently with them.

They took them to the hole in the church floor, Gad Beebe's place of interment. Seeing it again, Willow was shocked by what they had done, the violation they had caused.

'You did this?' grunted a man with sunken cheeks.

Boy was too fearful to speak after his last try. Willow couldn't see that there was any point in denying it, but couldn't bring herself to admit to it either.

Then Pitchfork Man spoke.

'What are we going to do with them?'

'Kill them now,' said one.

'We ought to send for the Watch,' said a taller man, who seemed nervous.

'That will take days,' said Pitchfork. 'Let's drown them in the mill race.'

'It's frozen, you fool! It'll take hours to make a hole big enough.'

And so they argued, and eventually decided to lock their prisoners in the crypt while they decided what to do.

The sunken-cheeked man pushed Boy and Willow ahead of him, waving his scythe threateningly. At the far end of the church, in a corner of the nave, was a low archway. Four steps led down from it to a metal grille. Sunken Cheeks, who seemed to have taken charge, had sent a younger man for the keys. When he returned he came back not just with the keys, but with women from the village, eager to see what was happening.

Sunken Cheeks pointed, unlocking the gate to the underworld.

Boy and Willow hesistated, but when he lowered the tip of his scythe at them they slunk into the darkness. Beyond the grille there were at least a dozen more steps that curved around, taking them back under the body of the church itself. At the bottom, they stopped. They had little choice, for they were in complete darkness.

There was a noise like a scuttling animal, then a flash of sparks behind them and they understood what the noise was – a burning torch had been thrown down the stairs so there was light to carry Valerian down.

He was dumped roughly on the floor.

'Heavy, he is,' said one, and they left. The nervous one turned and bent to take the torch back with them.

'Please!' said Willow. 'Please leave us some light!' She tried to make herself sound as pitiful as possible, but that wasn't hard. The man looked at her and was reminded of his own daughter sleeping safely in her bed in the farmhouse.

Without a word he handed her the torch and followed his friend back up the curving steps to the church.

Boy rushed after him, but the gate was already shut and locked.

'Please,' he begged through the metal grille of the crypt entrance, 'please can we have a blanket for Valerian?'

Sunken Cheeks looked at him.

'No,' he said.

Their footsteps disappeared up the four stone steps and they were gone.

3

The crypt was small, a cramped room with a vaulted ceiling low above their heads, which made it feel as if they were sitting inside a treasure chest. In the centre stood a large stone sarcophagus, and along each of the longer walls were three cists capped with headstones commemorating the person whose bones lay inside.

On one of the shorter walls was an iron bracket, and Willow put the torch there so that they could see a little better. Boy returned from the metal grille at the top of the steps.

'It's not good,' he said. 'It's locked tight.'

He shook his head.

'It's not like they need to stop people getting out of here, is it?'

'No,' said Willow. 'It's to stop people getting in. To stop them . . .'

'Stealing bodies,' said Boy, finishing what she was unable to.

'Boy,' cried Willow suddenly, 'what are we doing? What have we got into?'

'You, you mean,' said Boy. 'I was always a part of this. Whatever he does, I do. You had a choice.'

Willow looked at Valerian.

'Let's see what we can do for him.'

They lifted his head and folded the wide collar of his coat out, then rested his head back on it. His arm was worse. There was a distinctly unpleasant smell coming from it. They pulled his coat tight around him.

'Where's that last bottle?' said Willow.

Boy fished in Valerian's pockets and pulled out the last of Kepler's potion.

Lifting Valerian's head again, they tipped a small amount of the thin green liquid into his mouth.

Automatically he swallowed, coughing.

Boy sniffed the liquid before shoving the cork back. He pulled a face. As Willow was busy trying to lower Valerian's head, a burning curiosity came over him. Holding his nose, he took a small swig of the stuff.

He choked but swallowed. Immediately fire spread through his body. The taste was awful, but it was soon replaced by a wonderful feeling – a feeling of strength and power and lightness. He felt better than he had in days, in ages, and he liked it.

His body no longer ached. He felt no hunger, no pain, no fear. He looked at the bottle in his hand and then at Valerian, who already showed signs of stirring.

Willow turned round to Boy.

'What are you doing?' she asked.

'Nothing,' he said. 'Nothing.'

He smiled at Willow. Despite everything he was amazed to feel calm, confident, even *glad*.

'Well,' he said, 'what are we going to do?'

Willow crumpled in front of his eyes.

'What can we do?' she wailed. 'We're locked in a stone hole, underground, under a church, in a god-forsaken village miles from home. Valerian has two days left unless maybe we find the book, and we still have no idea where it is!'

She stopped.

'Don't we?' said a voice behind her.

Valerian looked up at them from the stones. He raised himself on one arm, then lifted himself back to his feet. Willow was amazed by this, but Boy no longer was. He knew the secret that was kept in Kepler's green liquid.

'Boy!' said Valerian, fishing in his pocket. 'Where's my bottle?'

'Here,' said Boy, bringing it to him. 'We just fed you a little of it. We thought it might help.' He couldn't hide the smile on his face as he saw Valerian on his feet again, and as Valerian took the bottle back from him with his good arm, he smiled back.

Boy felt good, strong and happy.

Valerian looked at the bottle. It was half empty.

'You were right,' he said, 'but there is little left. Still, it is time we were about things.'

He put a hand out to Boy's cheek for a moment, then seemed to remember himself and instantly pulled it back. It happened so fast that Boy wondered if he'd imagined it.

'But what can we do?' said Willow.

Valerian turned to her, his bad arm swinging loosely at his side.

'Come now, Willow, it's not like you to be weak! It's usually the boy here.'

Boy laughed. He didn't even mind Valerian making fun of him. He felt good and that was all.

Valerian began to circle the crypt. He prowled, a smile growing on his face.

'There is more to this church than we know,' he said. 'There has to be – it is far too big a place for a tiny hole of a village like Linden.'

He rested his hand on top of the sarcophagus.

193

'Listen!' he said. 'Listen! Can you hear it?'

Willow stared at him, convinced he had gone mad. Boy, who had spent a few more years with Valerian than Willow, recognised when his master was on to something.

'What?' he asked.

'Listen!' hissed Valerian, wobbling slightly on his feet. 'No! Look!'

He pointed at the wall of the crypt, the short wall opposite the one where Willow had placed the torch.

There again were those mysterious words.

Non omnem videt molitor aquam molam praeterfluentem.

'The miller . . . ?' began Boy.

'. . . sees not all the water that goes by his mill,' finished Willow.

'And outside the churchyard, there stands . . . Boy! What?'

'A mill!' he said confidently.

'Exactly!' declared Valerian.

'I don't understand,' cried Willow. 'What does it mean?'

'It means,' said Valerian, 'it means it is more than a motto! It is a family saying, maybe, but more than that. Listen! Place your ears to the sarcophagus and listen!'

'The – the what?' asked Boy.

'The sarcophagus, Boy! You do know what a sarcophagus is, don't you? From your Greek! Eater-of-bodies. Flesh-eater. Sarco-phagus.'

Boy looked blankly at him.

'The stone coffin, Boy!'

Valerian pointed to where Willow, who had already understood, stood on tiptoe to put her ear flat against the lid of the sarcophagus.

'I thought I heard something as I lay on the floor. It's faint, but you can hear it better through that.'

194

Boy ran over to Willow. It was true; you didn't even have to put your head close to the stone box to hear the sound of water flowing somewhere underneath.

'Valerian!' Willow said. 'Valerian! Look! Is this . . . ?'

She was staring at a pattern engraved in the lid of the coffin.

'Yes. The pattern that Kepler had dug into his cellar floor, repeated here on the lid of this supposed grave!'

Indeed, the lid of the sarcophagus was deeply cut with a manic pattern of lines crossing, re-crossing, intersecting and splitting. Without remembering exactly, Willow could recognise it.

Boy stared at her.

'What is it?' he asked.

'These marks,' she said. 'It's what the doctor had dug into his floor and filled with water. Water that flowed by the aid of a machine. And above it on the wall were those words.'

She pointed.

Boy understood.

'The mill outside – not all of the water goes past it. Some goes here. So the miller . . .'

'. . . sees not all the water that . . .'

'Exactly!' cried Valerian. He stared at them, a little mad, a little proud, waiting for the moment to deliver his final piece of wisdom.

'See that long line that comes out of the pattern, straight down the length of the sarcophagus lid?'

They nodded.

'What would you say that is, at the end of it? That symbol?'

There was a circle with short lines radiating out from it.

'It's a mill wheel!' said Boy.

'Just so!' said Valerian, and he grew more serious. 'Now, you two, lift the lid and let's be away from here!'

Willow turned to him.

'I am not dealing with any more corpses,' she said firmly. 'Is that clear? I've had enough!'

Valerian smiled at her infuriatingly.

'But there will be no corpse inside here,' he said, tapping the lid. 'There will be no bones, no flesh, no decomposing material of any sort whatsoever. There will be simply a way back to the City.'

'You're mad,' she said. Valerian ignored her.

'I thought Kepler was mad but I was wrong. I should have realised sooner what we were looking at in his cellar. This is a map. It is a map of the ancient canals under the City. And this is our way back.'

'That can't be,' said Boy. 'There are no canals in the City.'

'Not *in* the City, *under* it,' snapped Valerian. 'Under the City is an ancient network of canals. They were once exposed to the sky but were slowly bridged, then built over and re-built over, until only the rumour of them remains. I myself explored a tiny fraction of them one evil day when I was a student. I quickly became lost. It took me a day to find my way out and I never dared go back.

'It is said they feed into the river, or that the river feeds into them. Few know where their entrances lie. And now I believe we have found one, here, in this stinking village. The mill race must run underground and join the canals!'

Valerian fetched the torch from the wall.

'Hurry!' he said. 'There is no time to be lost.'

'But we don't even know if you're right,' protested Willow. 'There may be nothing inside here at all.'

'I am right,' said Valerian. 'And you two must open the lid. I cannot. Hurry!'

Willow looked at Boy, and Boy looked at Valerian, who glared at him so hard that he jumped and started to try to shift the heavy stone lid. It didn't budge.

'Wait!' said Valerian. 'We ought to copy this map.' He tapped the lid once more.

'I have some paper!' said Boy proudly, and pulled out a leaf of folded parchment from his pocket. Delighted at being useful for once, he smiled as Valerian took it from him.

'Boy, you astound me! What is this? Have you been studying at last, or . . . ?'

Valerian stopped.

'Where did you get this?' he said.

'It's mine!' said Boy, wishing he had left it in his pocket.

It was the paper he'd found on the viewing table of the camera obscura in the Tower room, the one with his name at the top and the strange words and symbols underneath.

'It is not yours,' shouted Valerian. 'It is *about* you.'

He turned and looked at Willow.

'Here,' he said. 'I have a stub of charcoal. Use the reverse of the paper to copy the map. Do it well!'

So by the flickering torchlight Willow set about trying to copy the lines on to the back of the paper, using a piece of soft charcoal that kept on breaking.

'I can't see!' she complained, but she kept at it.

'You've missed a bit,' said Boy. 'Look, there! And that line joins that one, not that one.'

'You do it if you're so—'

'Boy will not do it,' said Valerian, holding the torch. 'You will. You'll be quicker and neater.'

But it was hard to concentrate with Valerian glaring at her.

'Hurry!' he said. 'God knows how long those thugs will be away for.'

'They're just people,' said Willow. 'We offended them. They're angry. Perhaps if we had just asked to–'

'To what?' interrupted Valerian, 'Asked to smash a hole in the floor of their church and dig up the remains of one of the local gentry? I think you should concentrate on what you're doing.'

'There!' said Willow. 'I've finished.'

'Are you sure?' said Valerian, comparing the engraved lines with the drawing Willow had made.

'Yes,' said Willow, but she was not sure. She was not even convinced there was anything under the lid of the sarcophagus apart from decaying bodies.

'Then come on, put your backs into it. Don't take it right off – we must cover our tracks when we leave.'

But if Willow was not convinced, Boy certainly was. He still felt strong after the slug from the bottle. He had never felt so confident in his life, and had never felt he understood Valerian so well. It was as though some of *his* power was inside him.

'Come on, Willow, I need your help,' he said, putting his back against the lid and beginning to shove.

Reluctantly, Willow started to push too.

'Do it together!' urged Valerian. 'On my mark! Now!'

And they both gave a sudden shove and the stone lid not only moved but slid right off the sarcophagus and smashed to the stone floor of the crypt where it shattered.

The sound echoed around the small vault and they began to panic, casting anxious glances back up the steps. Valerian leant over into the hole they had uncovered and smiled, satisfied. There was a series of iron rungs let into the shaft that dropped down into the darkness. Now they could not only hear the sound of running water, they could smell its dankness.

'So much for covering our tracks,' said Valerian, looking at the broken lid. 'Still, we have a map, and if they follow, they won't have.'

'Why did they put us down here if they knew there was this way out?' asked Boy.

'Well, obviously they *didn't* know,' said Valerian. 'It's my guess this is some secret of the Beebe family. But we don't have time to debate it. They'll come sooner or later and the torch won't last for more than an hour or two. Let's go.'

He took a pull on the phial. As he lowered his head, he saw Boy staring at him.

'What is it, Boy?'

'I – I was just thinking, wondering whether it would be a good idea if Willow and I had . . . a little of that . . . to help us.'

'How dare you! No! What a suggestion! This is for my arm. Anyway, it's not good for you. Too much can . . . That's not your business. Take the torch and get down that hole, Boy, before I decide to leave you here.'

Boy tried to hide his disappointment and did as he was bid.

'You next, Willow.'

And then Valerian swung his long legs up on to the ledge of the shaft and placed his feet on the rungs. The light from the torch had already stopped swinging about beneath him.

Valerian was glad the bottom was not far. He had little idea how he would have managed if he'd had to climb down a ladder with only one hand for more than a few feet. As it was it was difficult enough, but quite soon he had reached the bottom and stepped off to find Boy and Willow waiting for him.

'Look!' said Boy. 'Boats!'

They were in a cavern, standing on a jetty made of iron

and wood which clung to the wall of the chamber. There was the river flowing slowly and steadily past them in the darkness, and tied to the jetty were several boats of a strange sort. They were flat-bottomed and had no oars, but each had a short pole lying in its bottom.

'I wonder when anyone last came this way,' said Willow. 'It feels so forgotten.'

It was true. The whole place seemed to have been untouched for many years. The rust on the iron rungs had been undisturbed. The landing stage was rotting in places, and they had to tread carefully to avoid the weaker parts of the platform, but the boats bobbed gently in the current, as if happy to see someone after years of abandonment in the darkness. They chose the one that seemed to be the sturdiest.

'Let's be gone,' said Valerian.

4

They began well.

The boat, once untied, seemed keen to take them off down the tunnel that led from the chamber, and only leaked a little. Willow sat at the front with the torch, Valerian sat in the middle with the map, giving orders, and Boy crouched in the back, holding the pole and steering them away from the walls when necessary. There was little need to propel them forward – the current was enough to keep them moving at a decent speed. Once or twice Boy gave an extra push, but he rocked the boat so badly it made them feel unsafe.

Soon they would be back in the City.

Time. Who had any idea how time was passing as they sailed along in the long straight tunnel?

Distance. They had no more idea about how far they had travelled than they had about how long they'd been going. What had seemed so easy to start with began to seem a surreal voyage from nowhere to nowhere. The tunnel was apparently endless.

As they went, Valerian's drugs began to wear off and the pain grew again in his arm. With it he began to remember the desperate nature of his situation.

So what if he made it back to the City? He knew what

waited for him on New Year's Eve, wherever he was. For the ten-thousandth time he wondered if there were any way out that he hadn't considered before. Maybe there was something staring him right in the face that he hadn't seen. But fifteen years is a long time to think and he had no more ideas.

They drifted on in the gloom, the torch sputtering, showing signs that it would soon fail.

It was not much warmer in the underground canal than it had been in the crypt, or in the church, or in the snowstorm itself. It was airless too. Despite the flowing water there was a powerful smell of dampness and decay. Once or twice their faces were brushed by dripping fronds and unseen tentacles, maybe the roots of plants hanging from the bricked vault of the low tunnel. The sound of splashes from the prow of the boat fell dead against the claustrophobic walls of the tunnel which, it seemed, would never end.

Valerian's mind was a haze of horror and pain. Boy began to feel his joy slip from him. He could see little but Willow by the light of the torch.

What had he brought her into? This life with the madman who was his master. He was possibly a murderer, whose life was now forfeit over something that had happened fifteen years before. Valerian had thrown it all away for one night with a woman who had rejected him.

Nothing made sense, especially not this stupidly straight tunnel.

'Boy,' said Willow quietly, 'I'm scared.'

'It's all right,' Boy said. 'It's . . .'

And then Willow shrieked and dropped the torch into the canal, where it was extinguished at once with a short hiss of dissent.

'Willow!' called Boy. 'Are you all right?'

'I dropped the torch,' she cried pointlessly. 'Something hit me! I'm sorry – oh, I'm sorry!'

'Are you all right?' Boy asked again.

'Yes, but what will we do now? We can't see where we're going!'

'What does it matter anyway?' said Boy. 'We're only going one way and that's forward. I don't know what else to do.'

'But we could be down here forever,' cried Willow.

The darkness was total, and still they floated on.

Valerian barely seemed to have noticed. Boy now gently eased himself into the bottom of the boat from his perch on the stern, and Willow, a little hysterical, felt her way back towards Valerian and curled up at his feet.

Then she sat up.

'I've still got a bit of a candle,' she called to Boy.

'But we've no way of lighting it,' he said miserably.

They fell silent again, and so they went, knowing little about anything, Boy and Willow half numbed by the cold and half asleep, and Valerian in some strange place where the pain and the last of the drugs had taken him.

5

Had they had any idea how time was passing they might have guessed that it was now well past midday on the day before New Year's Eve.

Had they any idea of how far they had travelled they might have known that they were indeed back in the City or, at least, beneath it.

Valerian was right. Valerian was always right. They were in the maze of underground canals that lay far from sight and far from knowledge, forgotten and corrupt, while the City sprawled above.

They had drifted into the canal system proper, where the current had become more gentle. Had they had any light to see by, they would have been able to make out ruined doorways and steps, landing stages and blocked in windows, where once a thriving business life had been conducted along the waterways of the City. Now the only life came from the water itself, gurgling and slurping its way towards various hidden gutters where it rushed unseen into the pestilent river that bisected the City itself.

Boy was half-awake now. Despite his exhaustion, he had been unable to sleep for long. There was too much fear running through his body to give him much peace. Valerian was unconscious again, Willow whimpering in her sleep like a disturbed dog at his feet. So it was only Boy who knew what happened when the boat suddenly struck something in the dark and came to a halt.

He put both hands out slowly into the darkness. The boat was resting against a low wall on his left. He could hear the sound of wood on wood in front of him. On the other the side of the boat he felt another prow under his fingers. He guessed rightly that the boat had hit another one moored at a landing point.

'Valerian!' he called as loudly as he dared. 'Willow! Wake up!'

He felt around the wall and found a crevice between two of the stones. He dug his fingers in and found it did not take much effort to keep their boat against the side. Keeping careful hold, he called out again.

'Valerian! Wake up! I think we might be able to get out. Willow! We're at some sort of jetty again. We're somewhere at last.'

'What is it?' came Valerian's voice from the darkness. 'Where are we? Why is it dark?'

'The torch went out,' said Boy. There was no need for Valerian to know that Willow had dropped it. 'It went out ages ago.'

'Where are we?' said Willow.

'What difference does it make?' asked Boy. 'It's dark everywhere.'

'No, it isn't,' said Willow. 'Look there!'

'Where?' asked Valerian.

In the dark it was impossible to know where Willow was looking, but then Boy saw.

Away to one side of them was a speck of light in a distant tunnel. It seemed to be very far away.

'Can you get out of the boat?' Valerian said.

'Who are you talking to?' asked Boy.

'Either of you!' Valerian barked, and his voice echoed around them, finally dying away after many beats of the heart. They were at the edge of some vast chamber, from across the far side of which came the faint light.

'I think I can,' said Willow, but Boy was already slithering over the side of the boat on to what turned out to be a quayside, long forgotten in this abandoned subterranean world.

'Find my hand,' said Willow, holding it out in the blackness.

Boy worked along the side of the quay, gripping the low edge of the boat, until his arm bumped into Willow's.

'Take the rope,' she said, passing it to Boy, who, fumbling around, found an iron ring to tie it to.

He pulled Willow up, and then they both helped lift Valerian out.

Once on firm ground, he seemed to recover and take charge again.

'We may as well head for the light. Perhaps it is coming in from the outside.'

And so they walked.

It was like walking on a black night, lit only by a few stars. They could make out their destination clearly enough, but the ground under their feet not at all.

On more than one occasion they caught their boots on rough ground and twice Willow was unlucky enough to walk into low stone bollards and fall over. It was an ancient square, which seemed to slope slightly uphill away from the canal, and with every step they could see more clearly that the light they were heading for was not daylight but artificial.

It was coming from a low archway in the corner of the

square, and beyond it a series of smaller arches that led into tiny tunnels, each half the height of an average man.

Boy and Willow hesitated, but Valerian strode through the entrance arch and then bent down at the opening of the small passage that now seemed to their eyes to be dazzling with light.

He jumped back.

The light wavered and then emerged from the hole. It was followed by a man.

'Valerian!' he gasped.

'Kepler!' spluttered Valerian.

6

Valerian and Kepler stood staring at each other, apparently unable to speak, then Kepler noticed the strange way Valerian was standing.

'What's happened to your arm?' he said.

'Broken,' said Valerian. 'I ran into Meade and his gang.'

'I warned you–'

'You warned me about a lot of things. But how are you here? The book! What about the book?'

'You would have done better to listen to me,' said Kepler, ignoring Valerian's question. 'If you had, you might not be in this mess.'

Kepler was thin, and dwarfed by Valerian. His receding hair lay in black straggles scraped across his head. He wore small glasses of his own design and manufacture. He was dressed in a black frock-coat and worn boots and his two gold teeth shone.

Boy and Willow were amazed by the light he was carrying. It was one of his own devices, without doubt. Slung over his shoulder on a wide canvas strap was a box with a brass handle protruding from it. From this one of his special wires connected to a wooden handle with a glass ball on the end. It was this glass ball that was glowing with a strong yellow light. From time to time the light weakened and Kepler would wind the handle on the box furiously. As he did so the light would return to its full strength.

Kepler walked over to Boy and Willow and inspected them by the light.

'Boy I know. Who is this?'

'A girl. Of some use. She's cleverer than Boy.'

Kepler grunted.

'What are you doing here?' he asked Valerian.

'No! Listen!' replied Valerian. 'Have you found the book?'

He grasped Kepler with his good hand.

Kepler sighed deeply.

'Alas, Valerian,' he sighed, 'I have not.'

'But what were you doing in there?' asked Valerian, pointing at the small tunnel from which Kepler had emerged.

Kepler hesitated just a fraction before answering.

'That was my last attempt,' he said. 'My investigations, on your behalf, led me down here. I was led to believe that the answer lay in these catacombs. It has not been easy. Finding a safe entrance to this world was hard enough. I succeeded, but now I have failed. I am sorry, Valerian. There can be no other way. You will have to face your future and your past tomorrow night.'

'But the motto!' Valerian cried. 'The Beebe motto led you down here?'

'Yes. The motto. That led me close. I learned that the Beebes knew of the catacombs. The family were advisors to the Emperor for many years. They came and went, from Linden to the Palace, through the canals. I thought the book was hidden here. It was not. You will have to face your past and your future tomorrow night.'

Valerian raged, cursing himself, cursing Kepler and Boy, cursing life itself. Again and again he cried, No! It seemed there would be no end to his anguish, but at last his rage spent itself and he fell silent. His head dropped.

'There is no other way,' Kepler said eventually. 'You know that. It is over after all.'

Valerian fell to his knees and did not move.

Boy put his hands to his head. What could he possibly say? Willow looked at Boy, then at Valerian.

'It can't happen!' she suddenly cried. 'You can't give up!'

Valerian remained motionless as she wrapped her arms around his head.

'Come on!' she cried. 'Boy, tell him.'

But Boy knew it was hopelesss and tears poured down his face. Kepler watched, motionless.

All four stayed that way for a long time.

Finally Kepler spoke.

'We should go. Back to the City.'

No one answered.

'There is no point staying down here,' he said.

'Not for you three,' said Valerian. 'You go. Leave me here.'

'We can't leave you,' cried Boy.

'It may as well happen here as anywhere,' said Valerian. 'There is no escaping it now. If I die here, at least no one will have to bury me.'

'No!' cried Boy. 'Don't give up!'

'I am not moving,' Valerian said. 'Give me the last of the medicine, Boy. Kepler, do you have any more of these with you? No? Never mind. I shall not be moving far now.'

He sat against a wall and bowed his head.

'I can't believe he's giving up,' Willow said to Boy, but Boy did not answer.

Kepler came and crouched by Valerian.

'Valerian! Listen! You will do what I say. You will come with me.'

'I will not! The only reason I like you is because you never preach at me, so don't start now. I am too ill and tired to move. I will stay here.'

Kepler got to his feet and gave his light another few cranks of the handle.

'Very well, he said. 'You leave me no alternative. I will not see you die in this way. I am going to mend your arm at least. I will take Boy, for help. The girl can stay with you.'

'But I don't want to go!' cried Boy

'And I don't want to leave Boy!' cried Willow.

'You will both do as I say,' said Kepler, 'for Valerian. I need Boy to help me carry things to mend his arm. Someone must stay with him.'

They argued a while longer, but Kepler would not be dissuaded and eventually Boy and Willow agreed. Valerian watched it all – it seemed to have no effect on him now.

Kepler had brought some torches in case his light device stopped working. He handed one to Boy and set it burning with a chemical match.

Then they left Willow and Valerian with Kepler's special light.

'Just turn the handle if it starts to fade,' Kepler instructed Willow. 'We'll be gone no more than a few hours.'

Then Boy and Kepler left for the boats.

As they went, Willow called after them, 'Don't be long!'

Her voice wavered in the darkness as they disappeared from view.

'Please.'

7

Kepler held the torch over the prow of the boat. He seemed not to need a map. Boy sat in the back of the boat and they followed the natural flow of the canal towards one of the river inlets, but making two difficult turns. Boy was not sure he could find his way back to Willow and Valerian if Kepler were not with him.

'Doesn't really take that long,' said Kepler over his shoulder. 'You just have to know which way to go, or you could be in here forever.'

He laughed. It was not a nice laugh.

Kepler called out more directions and Boy obeyed.

'Did you know the girl well?' said Kepler.

What did he mean, 'Did'? thought Boy.

'Willow's a friend of mine,' he said. There was a note of surprise in his voice, as if he himself were only now realising this. But it felt right saying it. 'A good friend.'

'And bad about Valerian, too,' Kepler went on. 'It can't be helped though. It has to be like this.'

'What are you talking about?' asked Boy, shipping the pole into the boat. They drifted.

'That I found the book. Oh yes, I found it days ago, but when I saw – well, I knew I had to hide it again. I was just hiding it when you and Valerian and the girl arrived. That

212

was your good fortune. If he had found it! Well. Shame they'll have to die. Although I suppose the girl *might* find her way out. That's why I left her the lamp, but otherwise . . .'

Boy felt himself go cold. Then fear and anger rushed through him. He was sitting in a boat with a madman. Kepler seemed to think Valerian was the enemy and that he had to hide the book from him, not find it for him.

Kepler rambled on.

'I have known him a long time, but then he deserves no better after all he's done. We will have to get along without him!'

He laughed again, then peered ahead into the gloom.

'A left coming up, I think. Yes. Boy? A left! A left!'

But Boy had another use for the pole. He took careful aim and swiped Kepler around the head with it. His aim was true and Kepler fell clean over the side into the water.

To Boy's good fortune, the torch dropped inside the boat.

Boy started to push the boat hard against the current. He had to find his way back to Valerian. His life depended on it, and Boy was not going to let him down.

'Valerian!' he called into the darkness. 'I'm coming. I'm coming!'

Behind him, Kepler sunk under the water for a moment then, as the cold revived him, came spluttering to the surface.

'Boy!' he coughed. 'Boy! Come back! Boy! You don't understand! Come back!'

But he could only gasp the words, and Boy was already far away.

8

Boy hurried back to his master. Some strange power entered him, and he remembered without hesitation every turn he had made in the dark. The torch guttered on its side in the bottom of the boat, and the wood where it lay started to smoulder, but Boy fixed his eyes on the tunnels ahead, until he was back at the quayside of the underground square.

He leapt from the boat and ran across the square, holding the torch in front of him.

'Valerian! Willow! Valerian! Valerian!'

Willow lifted her lamp high and scrambled to her feet as he arrived.

'Valerian! I know where the book is! I know!'

Now even Valerian was roused from his stupor.

Boy ran right to the entrance of the low tunnel where Kepler had emerged and pointed.

'The book's in there! Kepler's crazy! He was trying to hide it from us! I wouldn't let him do that. I hit him! Maybe I – I don't know, but I *can't* let you go, Valerian.'

Valerian almost leapt to his feet, despite his arm.

'Kepler . . .' he murmured to himself. 'Kepler! I was wrong to think the past was the past. I, of all people, should know that!'

He looked at Boy.

'You have done well,' he said, his eyes shining with a renewed power. 'I am pleased with you.'

Boy stood, speechless.

'Now!' said Valerian. 'Give me the light, Willow. I'm going inside.'

Valerian got down on his hands and knees, and shoving the lamp ahead of him, he crawled into the tunnel, moving along like a three-legged dog.

Boy turned to Willow.

'I think I've killed Kepler,' he said.

Willow said nothing. Boy did not stop, could not stop. The words tumbled from his mouth.

'He was just leaving you here to die with Valerian. I didn't think. I just did it.'

'What did you do?' Willow asked.

'I hit him with the pole. He went into the water. I–'

'Boy . . .' she stopped, then held her hand out to him. 'Let's hope the book gives Valerian the answer he needs. Then it may have been worth it.'

Boy sat down with Willow to wait. They leant against each other in the dank air and watched the flame of the torch flicker and spark. Its smoke twisted away to the low ceiling of the passage from which the many smaller tunnels led.

'It's going out,' said Boy.

'No, it isn't,' Willow said firmly. 'It can't be.'

But it was. They tried to turn the torch this way and that, to coax the flame back into life, but they only seemed to be making it worse. It went out, and they held each other, trying not to panic.

'He'll be back soon,' said Boy. 'Soon.'

They waited.

Eventually they heard a sound, and saw the light flooding the entrance.

Valerian emerged, triumphant. He backed out of the low tunnel, dragging something behind him. It was a huge book, vastly ancient and tattered beyond belief. There was a strange expression on Valerian's face as he clutched it. A look of joy. Stronger than joy – it was joy and delight and rapture and hope combined. His eyes burned at Boy and Willow, and then at the thick tome grasped in his strong fingers.

'Is that it?' asked Boy, though there was no need.

It was undoubtedly what they had been looking for for so long. At last the weight was too much for Valerian to hold in one hand and he put the book on the ground in front of him.

'Now let us see . . .' he said, his voice quiet and strangely high.

He lifted the book so it balanced on its spine.

'Wind this infernal contraption for me, will you?' he said to Willow. 'Good. Now hold it there.'

Valerian let the book fall open, as if letting it choose which page it would show to him, what secrets it would impart to him.

Boy stared as Valerian flicked backwards and forwards through the book, searching for his answer. None of them moved, save for Valerian occasionally turning a page and Willow winding the light whenever it began to fail.

Valerian's face drew closer to the book as he seemed to find what he was looking for. Or was it that the book was showing him what it wanted to show him?

Willow, holding the lamp, tried to read what she could, but the book was written in many different and strange languages, and she could only understand a few words.

Suddenly Valerian gripped the edges of the book so

tightly Boy thought he might pull it apart. He leant closer, his hands shaking.

With fumbling fingers he delved deep into his coat pocket and pulled out a piece of paper – a piece of paper that Boy immediately recognised as the one Kepler had written about him, on the back of which Willow had copied the map.

Now Valerian began to pore over this paper as well as a certain page of the book, and a frown spread across his face and then vanished just as easily.

He looked up.

'Boy,' he said quietly, 'I have my answer.'

'What – what is it, Valerian?' Boy asked.

'You. You are my answer,' Valerian said, grinning.

Willow, who had been silently trying to read the book over Valerian's shoulder, suddenly gasped. She was not even trying to decipher the peculiar words any more, but somehow there was knowledge in her head – a picture that filled her mind with horror.

'Oh . . . Boy!' she yelled. 'He wants to kill you! Boy! Run!'

The grin slipped from Valerian's face as he swung his arm and punched Willow hard in the face. She dropped to the ground, spilling the light. She did not move.

Valerian turned to Boy.

'There's nothing to be scared of,' said Valerian smoothly, his voice calm. 'Come here. There's nothing wrong. Come closer.'

But Boy did not come closer.

He took a quick, faltering glance at Willow's still body on the stone flags, and then he turned and ran.

217

December 31st – New Year's Eve

The Day of
Absolute Promotion

❧

Boy ran automatically, without thinking, without realising what he was doing. He ran off into the darkness, and only after some time of running blindly did he realise that he had no light to run by. He stopped. Everything was inky around him, and now he found himself paralysed by the darkness. He felt unable to move without seeing where it was he was moving to.

He was aware of a light behind him.

He had gone perhaps fifty paces into the gloom across the square. He turned, and with alarm saw that Valerian was following, though slowly. He was walking unevenly, almost staggering.

He doesn't know where I am, Boy thought.

Boy could see Valerian clearly enough. He had grabbed Kepler's light device from beside Willow's body and was heading in the direction he thought Boy had gone. But blinded somewhat by his light, he could not see far enough into the gloom to see Boy.

All this passed through Boy's head in a flash.

He could see Valerian because of the light, and it was enough to dimly pick up a little of the shapes of old buildings around him. If he was careful, very careful, Boy guessed he might be able to use Valerian's own light to see his way, and provided he kept as far from Valerian as the faint light would allow, Valerian would have no idea where he was.

He would have to be careful – if he judged it wrong, Valerian would see him.

Nervously, Boy began to edge backwards and tripped over a low stone kerb. He fell with a groan and saw Valerian freeze. Boy watched in horror as Valerian held the lamp higher, away from his face, and looked right at where Boy sat on his backside.

'Boy!' called Valerian. 'Come here, Boy.'

Boy scrambled to his feet and scuttled further into the darkness.

'There you are!' cried Valerian, and started to follow, more quickly this time.

Boy hurried on and as silently as he could began to circle around sideways from his last position.

Crouching low to the pavement, Boy watched as Valerian moved straight on ahead, unaware of where he was. The tall man looked demonic as he passed within a few yards of Boy. His face was illuminated from underneath by the lamp, picking out its shadows and crevices.

'Boy!' called Valerian. 'I know you're there, Boy.'

But it was clear that he did not.

This was better. Boy waited until Valerian had passed him and gone a fair way ahead, and then began to follow him.

Perhaps, eventually, Valerian would lead him to the outside. Or maybe they would pass within sight of a channel of daylight, if indeed it was day outside, and then Boy could find his own way out.

He had no idea what time it was or what day it was, and maybe only Valerian knew, somehow, deep inside, that his last day had arrived.

Indeed, a few stone feet above their heads midnight had

come and gone and the early hours of New Year's Eve were starting to unwind across the length and breadth of the City. Most people were shut up fast in their beds, trying to sleep as deeply as possible to prepare for the manic celebrations that would entwine the City that night to welcome in the new year.

Boy crept along behind Valerian, who called ahead of him into the darkness.

'Boy. Boy! Are you there? Come here, Boy. I won't hurt you.'

2

Willow woke and began to panic. There was not the slightest suspicion of light anywhere, and the more she strained to see something – anything at all – and failed, the worse she felt. She couldn't believe there could be no difference between having her eyes open and shut and realised what it must be to be blind. She felt like screaming, but remembered that Valerian was out there in the blackness somewhere, his mind set on murder.

Murder? Was that really what she'd seen in his eyes when he'd read the book and found his answer? It was hard, but maybe not impossible to believe. She had been looking over Valerian's shoulder, trying to understand the strange writing and symbols. She had seen the piece of paper about Boy, too, but it was not these things that had told her.

No. That knowledge had simply appeared in her head as she looked at the pages of the book. She had seen what Valerian intended for Boy. The book had *shown* it to her.

If that was not evidence enough, the blow he had struck her was. Why else would he silence her so brutally? She felt her face in the darkness. Her eye hurt. She thought she could feel the stickiness of blood on her fingers.

She heard a sound, and tensed.

A low, grating noise. She tried to place it, to identify its source and direction, but she could not. Everything was disorientating without sight. Again she wanted to scream, and to be sick from the fear, but she fought the impulse.

She tried to breathe more deeply and slowly. She listened again, thinking she had perhaps imagined it. But no, there it was again, coming closer and getting louder.

She tried to decide what to do but found herself struggling to think clearly. She could try and crawl away from the noise but that would be difficult, and where could she go? Maybe it was better to stay where she was – she couldn't see whatever it was that was making the noise so maybe it couldn't see her either. Maybe. If, on the other hand, it was some *thing* from the canal, it would be used to moving in darkness. Perhaps it could even see in the dark and was coming right for her.

She heard a different noise, a small scraping sound, and saw – or maybe she only imagined it – the briefest spark of light. The light, had it been there at all, was gone, and she thought she heard a voice.

She sprang to her feet. Her head throbbed from Valerian's fist and she felt dizzy. Stumbling against some unseen pavement in the blackness, she fell.

She let out a groan as she hit the ground, her wrists taking the fall.

'Boy?' came a voice. 'Willow?'

Willow lay still, her head pounding, her breath coming short and fast. Her face was inches from the stone flags and she could feel their dampness seep into her.

She noticed that the sound had stopped.

'Willow?' came the voice from the darkness. 'It's me. It's Kepler.'

Willow was too surprised to say anything. Kepler, who had left her to die with Valerian, was not who she would

225

have chosen to have found her. Boy had half-killed him, trying to save . . . Valerian, who was lurking somewhere, threatening death in the dark.

There was nothing else to do.

'Kepler!' she called out. 'It's me, Willow!'

'Where are you, child? Is Boy with you? I fear for his safety.'

'What about my safety?' asked Willow bitterly.

There was no reply.

'Well?' said Willow again in the dark.

'You are safe,' Kepler said. 'You are safe from Valerian. It is only Boy who can save him. Only Boy's life is in danger. We would have come back for you–'

Willow cut him short.

'Oh! I don't believe you!'

'I swear,' said Kepler, 'I swear you were safe. The danger lies only to Valerian and to Boy. Once Valerian had . . . gone, I would have returned for you.'

'I don't understand,' said Willow, hesitating. 'I don't understand any of it. I don't know what I'm doing. I don't know where Boy is . . .'

'Yes,' said Kepler, 'we have to find Boy. He's the one in danger.'

'Why?' asked Willow. 'What does Valerian want him for?'

'I will explain,' said Kepler, 'but let me find you first. Where are you?'

'I don't know,' said Willow. 'Where are you?'

'Over here,' said Kepler. 'I have some matches but they are a little damp . . .'

Willow heard the noise she had heard before – the small scraping sound and then a fizz of sparks, which rapidly died away.

'Wet. Where are you?'

Willow nearly laughed in spite of herself, in spite of the horror which she found herself in.

The louder noise started again and Willow knew that Kepler was getting closer. She didn't like the idea, but equally she didn't like the thought of being alone in darkness any more.

'That's it,' she said. 'I'm this way. Yes, this way.'

And then Kepler bumped into her foot.

'That's close enough,' she said. 'Now, tell me what is going on.'

3

It was working, after a fashion.

Boy crawled on his hands and knees a handful of paces
behind Valerian, who made slow progress. In fact, Valerian
was walking more and more slowly all the time. Boy wondered if he was getting tired, or if his arm was giving him
more pain, but whatever the reason, Boy found it no trouble
at all to keep up with him, even crawling as he was.

Slowly they made their way on through the catacombs.
Occasionally they would come across a branch of the canal,
gurgling gently, the water an oily black snake that shugged
off into the next section of tunnel.

Now they were in a long corridor, a straight path with
a low ceiling composed, Boy supposed, of buildings that
soared away into the City above their heads, into the long-
forgotten daylight.

It was an unsettling world. Far underground, this deserted
empire lurked unknown to almost everyone. Boy was now
following Valerian down a low tunnel in which sound
behaved strangely. There was an echo from the scrape of
Valerian's boots, but it was a short, dry sound, cut off almost
as soon as it had begun. The ceiling hung with miniature
stalactites, at the end of which were small, ice-cool drops of
water. When one of these fell on to Boy's neck it was all he

could do to stop himself from shrieking and giving himself away. And then there was the smell of the place – musty, damp, full of spores of unseen fungus noiselessly swelling in the lightless passages and caverns.

They passed a gateway – an iron gate, with a massive rusty iron lock. Behind it the darkness stretched away into depths that no one would ever see.

Along each side of the corridor were low doorways, and at each one of these Valerian would stop a few feet short.

As Boy passed them, there was still enough light from Valerian's lamp to see strange numbers over the lintels, carved and then painted. The numbers made no sense to Boy, but some of the doorways bore inscriptions instead. *Sometimes*, said one, *it is better to die than to live.*

Oh good! thought Boy. *Just the sort of thing Valerian will love.*

Then he saw something which bothered him, though he couldn't work out why. Valerian began to scratch his nose in a nervous way. For a long time Boy watched, trying but failing to work out what it was that upset him about this.

Boy scratched his nose.

Valerian peered into the doorways. Suddenly he dropped his pace near to a dead halt and tiptoed the last inches to the doorway, swinging the lantern round in a rush.

'Boy?' he called into each doorway, and something in his voice made Boy's skin creep. He hung back further from Valerian's light, until he was sure he would not be seen by his master.

Valerian moved on.

'Boy!' he called. 'Boy, I know you're there. Come out. Let's talk. There's really nothing to be scared of. I need your help.'

Boy didn't want to listen, but had no choice. He crawled

229

on after Valerian, all the time hoping that he would see a way out, maybe a patch of light or a breeze of fresh air.

Valerian had stopped. The light from the device was failing and he could not carry it and wind the handle at the same time. He placed the box on the ground and, steadying it with his foot, he leant down and began to wind the handle evenly, looking about as he did. The light from the globe shone strongly again, and Valerian picked it up.

'I don't want to hurt you,' Valerian said, and Boy thought about Willow and wondered if she was dead. If she wasn't, he shouldn't have left her. But what could he do? He had had to run, or Valerian would have had him. Broken arm or not, he would have had him, of that Boy was sure. Valerian always got what he wanted. Always.

'Come out, Boy. I know you're there. Come out, Boy. I need your help. Haven't I helped you all these years?'

Valerian sounded tired. He sounded old and pathetic and sad, and Boy wished he would be quiet.

'I found you. In the streets I found you, grovelling in dark places. I gave you a life, and a place to sleep and food. We've come a long way, Boy, you and I, haven't we?'

Boy thought about just how far he'd come. Here he was, still grovelling around in dark places. Well, at least that was familiar ground. He watched as Valerian slid up to another of the low doorways and repeated his trick of stealing the last inches on tiptoe. Finding nothing, he moved on.

'I've always looked after you, haven't I, Boy? Yes, I have. But now I need you to help me. That's not so much to ask, is it? You know I'm in trouble, Boy, don't you? You know I need help. You are my famulus! I need *your* help, Boy. You're the only one who can help me now.'

Boy listened as Valerian drawled on, his voice full of pain and pitiful to hear.

Boy found himself crying in the darkness.

'Please, Boy. Come out. We can go on as we did before. I'm not going to hurt you, Boy. I need you. You don't know how much you mean to me. And besides, there are things I've never told you – things I should tell you. About who you are, where you came from. You'd like to know about who you really are, wouldn't you?'

Now Boy was listening hard. Valerian couldn't know anything about his parents, could he? But supposing he did? What if Valerian died and he never found out?

'Yes, I can tell you who you are, Boy. I can tell you about your father, your mother. So come out and let me talk to you.'

Boy stood up. Valerian could not yet see him, but Boy began to walk slowly, his heart thumping in his chest, towards the light.

'I do need your help. And I can tell you who you are, Boy. Who you are, and where you came from.'

Now Boy stood a few feet behind Valerian.

'Who am I, Valerian?' he asked quietly.

Valerian jerked round and lifted the light high, making sure it was really Boy he was looking at.

'Boy!' he shouted. 'There you are! Come on, there's no time to lose!'

But Boy stood still, and though his blood beat through his veins as if they would burst, he spoke calmly to his master.

'I'm not going anywhere, Valerian, until you tell me who I am.'

Valerian took a step towards Boy, his face blank.

'I give the orders, Boy, you know that. Now come here. I won't hurt you.'

Boy took another step backwards.

'Who am I, Valerian?' he cried. 'You said you'd tell me.'

'Boy,' growled Valerian, coming closer, and for the first time Boy faltered. He could see Valerian's eyes more clearly now, he could feel them eat into his own, finding their way into his mind, making him feel so small, so helpless. He would do anything Valerian told him. He always had, he always would . . .

With an effort, Boy wrenched his eyes away and ran several steps back into the shadows.

'Come here,' said Valerian. 'Come here!'

'No,' said Boy.

'Come here!' Valerian shouted, his face filled with rage and frustration. 'You! Boy! Come here!'

Boy turned and ran into the nearest doorway that led from the corridor.

Valerian's light bobbed after him.

4

'But what can we do?' Willow said.

'We need to find a light', said Kepler, 'or we shall die down here. Let me try another match now. The warmth from my hands may have dried them a little.'

This time there was a stronger flicker of flame that lasted longer but died as it reached the wood of the match.

In that short time Willow saw Kepler had a cut above his right ear, a vivid slash of red across his face. He stared at the failing match intently, his desperation clearly visible.

'What happened to your head?' asked Willow. 'Did you fall?'

'In a way,' he answered. 'Never mind that now. It happened when Boy and I parted company in the canals.'

'But the canals . . . ?'

'Are not deep. No more than waist-high in most places. You need to watch your step occasionally. There's one place a little further along where—'

'But why were you coming down here? To find the book?'

'No,' said Kepler, and he laughed, a snorting noise that Willow hated him for. 'No! I came down here to hide it.'

Now Willow was confused.

'To hide it? To hide it?'

'Yes. You see, Willow, I learnt things. I have been helping

Valerian for a long time. We had not seen each other since . . . for years, until one day he just arrived at my house and told me about the spectre he faced. He turned up as if nothing had ever happened between us! But when he told me about the book, I knew I would put the past behind me. Now is not the time, and certainly not the place to tell you all the trials and troubles we faced, attempting to find the book. Suffice to say that I discovered that an answer would be contained therein.'

'But what is the book? What did you learn?'

'It is an almanack, but much more than that. It holds answers to questions that men ask. It holds information about all manner of dealings, both light and dark. It contains much information on the nature of the . . . agreement into which Valerian placed himself. And it answers questions – questions in the mind of the reader. It could solve Valerian's problem – of that there is no doubt.'

'You mean–'

'Yes, I mean exactly that. Valerian's life ending in a most horrible way.'

Willow thought of something that had been bothering her. Something important.

'Why?' she asked.

'What?' Kepler replied.

'You were supposed to be helping Valerian find the book. And now you're telling me you've been trying to hide it from him. Why?'

'I thought you had realised that. The horoscope. Boy's horoscope. That gave me the answer, really.'

'What's a–?'

'Horoscope? It's a method of thinking about people, based on the patterns of the stars and the planets. It explains who people are, and why they are. It has deep scientific basis which few men truly understand, and yet the results of such investigation can be powerful.

'It concerns the heavens. The stars and the planets and their motions around the Sun, which is the centre of the universe, and their relative motions around the Earth.'

'I don't understand,' said Willow, feeling lost and lonely again.

'That doesn't matter. Just understand this. The position of all these things in the sky at the moment of an individual's conception determines the nature, the character, of that individual. Irrevocably.'

Now Willow began to understand.

'The piece of paper Valerian found, with Boy's name on it – is that his horoscope?'

'Sort of,' said Kepler. 'Sort of.'

'But how can you have worked these things out about Boy? You said you have to know where the planets were at the moment someone was born, but you can't have known that for Boy. No one knows when he was born – not even he does!'

'I made a guess. I felt a coincidence. An enormous coincidence, maybe, or Fate working its path through Boy and Valerian's lives. And mine, too. And then I found the book, and the book confirmed it. It *showed* me. I found out the truth of things.'

'But what is this coincidence?' asked Willow.

'That two people have come to be together. In all this sprawling city of tens of thousands, that two people should find each other. No, I think it is not coincidence. I think this is how Fate works.'

'So why were you trying to hide it? I still don't understand . . .'

'Valerian will kill Boy,' said Kepler. 'That is the answer.

235

That is the only way he can save himself now – for him to give Boy's life in place of his own. The pact can be broken only by a life exactly as long as the term of the bargain. That is what I discovered. I guessed much of this. The book confirmed it to me. I guessed who Boy is, and when he was conceived, and I drew up his horoscope. I found that it described the boy I knew very well. And so then, knowing who Boy is and having looked into the book, I knew what Valerian would do if he found out. And so I began to try to hide the path I had started to clear. I came down here to hide the book.

'In a few hours from now Valerian can offer Boy in place of himself, and he will go free. That is how and why Valerian will kill Boy. That is why we have to find Boy before Valerian does.'

Willow's heart thumped inside its rib-prison.

Boy. Valerian would kill Boy to save himself. Finally she began to understand the insane nature of the journey they had all been making. A dance – a hideous dance with Fate and Death.

Something else occurred to her.

'But why do you care about Boy?' she asked.

'Why do you?' said Kepler.

Before Willow could answer, Kepler spoke again.

'I have my reasons, as I'm sure do you. And I want the book.'

'So where did you find it?' Willow asked, 'Who does it belong to?'

'I heard, after years of searching far and wide, that it had been in the possession of a rich and powerful family. A family who lived in the City itself. A family called Beebe.'

In the darkness, Willow jumped at the name, but Kepler continued unaware.

'A large and powerful family, though corrupt and broken

236

now. They once owned properties in the City, and a large estate in the countryside. They built a church there, as their private place of worship, and eternal rest. That was where I found the book.'

'Where?'

'In Gad Beebe's grave. I had traced it as far as the Beebes. A sum of money to one of their more degenerate members, and the book's whereabouts became mine . . .'

'But . . .' Willow felt her head swimming, 'But I don't understand.'

'What?' asked Kepler.

'Gad Beebe. We looked in Gad Beebe's grave – there was nothing in there but his bones . . . you must have got there before us.'

Now it was Kepler's turn to be surprised.

'You went to Linden? You went to Beebe's grave? But how? How did you know his name?'

Willow smiled.

'I worked it out, from the music box that Boy got from Green. I don't know where Green had got it from, but the notes of the tune it played spelled his name. Gad Beebe.'

In the darkness Kepler started to laugh, bitterly. Then he stopped abruptly.

'But that is too ridiculous.'

'What?' asked Willow.

'That music box . . . I found it in Beebe's grave. I gave it to Green. Me! I'd brought it back from Linden. It amused me. Then I sent for Green, I needed him to go and meet Valerian. He saw it on my desk, and asked what it was. When I showed him he smiled like a child. He asked for it, along with the money I was paying him. He refused to do the job unless I gave it to him. That thug! But it was nothing to me, so I gave it to him. He must have had it with him when he went out to meet Valerian in The Trumpet.'

'But it held Gad Beebe's name!' cried Willow. 'Without it we'd have never found the grave . . .'

'Fate, once more,' Kepler said, 'Fate steering us all for its own ends . . .'

Willow thought about what he'd said. It did seem extraordinary. That little music box had made its way from Gad Beebe's grave, to Kepler and Green to Boy to Valerian, and only she had known what it held. Without it Valerian would still be struggling for the answer, and Boy would be safe. It was a coincidence too great to be anything other than true. The true path of Fate.

Then something occurred to her.

'But why?' she asked. 'Why did you send Green to meet Boy, in The Trumpet?'

'I sent him to meet Valerian – did he send Boy instead? That may have saved his life.'

'What do you mean?' asked Willow.

'I was supposed to meet Valerian that evening, to report any progress on the book. He knew I was close to finding it. In fact, I already had the book, and had read it. I'd learnt what it would mean for Valerian. For Boy. So I had to send Green instead. I sent a letter to Valerian at the theatre, telling him to meet Green.'

'But what did you tell Green to say to Valerian? He was expecting to get some news from you.'

'I didn't tell him to say anything, I told him to kill him.'

Willow froze.

'Yes, Willow, I told him to kill him. In another few days he'd be dead anyway, and I knew if he found the book that Boy's life would be in danger.'

'But he's your friend! You've known him for years. Worked with him! You couldn't just have him killed!'

'We were friends. Once, a long time ago, maybe. Then we fell out. We became rivals. He . . . hurt someone, someone I cared for. He betrayed me. Around the time he was expelled by the Academy. We didn't see each other for ten years. Then he came to ask for my help, but we were never friends again . . . He told me about the book. And I wanted it. I was never interested in helping Valerian, I wanted the book.'

'I still don't believe it,' Willow said, fiercely.

'Listen, girl,' cried Kepler, growing angry. 'It's him or Boy now. Understand that! Only one of them can live! And I want it to be Boy . . .'

They sat in silence for a long time, until all the questions in Willow's head fought to be answered.

'So, what did you do then? After Linden? Did you use the tunnel to get here?'

'Tunnel?' asked Kepler.

'It's how we got here,' Willow said, 'We found the entrance to a tunnel in the crypt of the church, and an underground river that led all the way here.'

'I thought it was maybe so,' said Kepler. 'During my researches into the book, I found a map of all the catacombs and canals. I made a model of them in my cellar, to try to learn the routes by heart. It is only because I did, that I was able to find my way back here in the dark.'

'In your basement? The canals and the writing?'

Kepler nodded in the darkness.

'But I did not have time to investigate while I was in Linden. To see if I was right about a tunnel all the way out there. It was built by the Beebes, when they were most powerful, as a link to the heart of the City. That tunnel is much newer than the rest of this place.'

'So you came back to the City overland?'

'Yes, I had hired a horse. I had the book. I'd found the book in the grave, and the music box there, too, and brought them both back from Linden, but it took me a long time. When I got back to the City, things had become complicated. Valerian's house is being guarded by the Watch. And there have been deaths, I understand.'

Willow was silent.

'Yes, I know about the deaths,' Kepler said. 'I heard about Green, though we may never know exactly what happened that night. I went to The Trumpet yesterday. And Korp, too.'

'Who told you?' Willow asked.

'Korp's murder is big news,' said Kepler.

'Valerian? Was it Valerian who did it?'

'I have no idea. Even I cannot work out everything that is going on here. I wonder where the book is now. Valerian must have taken it with him.'

'I don't know that he has,' said Willow. 'He can't carry that and the light, can he?'

'True.'

'But what about the paper? The horoscope? Valerian found it in your desk.'

'The horoscope. So, I made another mistake! I think I left it there, in my hurry to get to Linden. Well, that was as good as handing Valerian a key, but it would still not have been any use had he not found the book. That was why I had to get him away from here. When you three found me, I was hiding the book. Valerian was terrified of this place. He came down here once as a student. He got lost and nearly died. He vowed never to come here again. I thought this the best place to hide it.'

'You could have burned it. Thrown it in the river!'

240

'I could no more do that than cut off my own hand!' cried Kepler. 'I want the book when Valerian is . . . I want the book. It is full of all knowledge. It holds enormous power, as the success of the Beebe family demonstrates. But more than that, it shows things to the reader, things only about them and their destiny . . .'

'But if it is so great a thing, so powerful, then why did the Beebes bury it with Gad?'

'Apparently they thought it dangerous. That its power was not always . . . good. That it could corrupt.'

Willow shivered.

'Are you sure it's safe to use it?' she began, but Kepler cut her off.

'Of course!' he said dismissively. 'The Beebes were fools. They used it unwisely and their downfall was the result. So they decided to hide the book. But in the right hands . . . it's nonsense to suggest it could do anything other than impart wisdom.'

They sat without speaking as Kepler's last words drifted away into the darkness around them. Willow began to panic.

'And we still have no light,' she said desperately.

'No,' agreed Kepler, 'we do not.'

'No!' cried Willow suddenly. 'No. I mean, maybe we do.'

She rummaged around in her coat. In her pocket she found the candle stub they had used in the great cemetery, and later in Kepler's house.

'Why didn't I remember before?' Willow wailed, though in truth it would have been no use without a source of flame to light it from.

'What is it?' asked Kepler, unable to see what she was doing.

'I have a bit of a candle,' she explained. 'Maybe you could try one more match and see if we can get it alight.'

241

'Excellent,' he said.

She heard him move and then felt him put out his hands.

'Where's the candle?' he said. 'Hold still, stay close. Right.'

Again the match flared briefly, and before the head could burn away, he held it to the wick of Willow's candle stub. It took, and a small glow grew about them.

The relief was enormous, though the tiny patch of light only seemed to reinforce the oppressive gloom.

Now Kepler saw Willow's face.

'Your face?' he asked.

Willow nodded.

'Yes,' she said. 'Valerian.'

'We must find Boy.'

Then, in the light of the candle, which Kepler had taken from Willow and was shielding with one hand, they saw something else.

'The book!' Willow cried.

'That is good fortune. Our luck is turning. That is often how Fate works. One piece of good fortune begets another. Now come on! To your feet! I can get us out of here, but first we *must* find Boy!'

5

It had been a mistake to show himself to Valerian, and Boy knew it. How could he trust Valerian any more? How could he? Valerian was probably already a murderer. Korp or Green – or both? No, he couldn't have killed them both.

What was certain was that Boy could not trust himself with Valerian. Just to be held by his eyes for a moment too long was to forget right and wrong, to mistake black and white.

The game of cat and mouse resumed, but now with Valerian pursuing Boy rather than Boy trailing his master. Valerian was unable to travel fast, and the tunnel was low. He walked hunched over the lamp. The tunnel Boy had chosen was small and straight and narrow, and Valerian could clearly see Boy ahead of him, hurrying away.

Sickeningly, Boy knew this, and he scuttled along as fast as he could.

And then, abruptly, the roof lifted away above his head and Boy stood in a vast open space, though still far beneath the City streets. There were small hills in front of him, it seemed – piles of whiteness in the gloom. As he heard Valerian coming closer, nearing the edge of the tunnel, Boy realised that he had stopped at the threshold of this new space.

Valerian approached, and as he did, the light intensified. Boy lurched forward, missed his footing, and stumbled into one of the piles of white stuff. It was hard, but scattered under his weight. He could hear things cracking. Valerian emerged from the tunnel and shone the light straight at Boy.

'So!' he cried. 'I have you at last.'

In the light Boy realised he was sitting in piles of bones. Human bones of all sorts. He knew they were human by the large number of skulls rolling around at his feet.

He screamed.

As Valerian came closer, Boy picked up a skull and threw it. Valerian ducked but was too slow, and the ancient head-bone hit his bad arm. He howled, and wavered where he stood. In that split second Boy scrambled clumsily to his feet, bones skidding away under him, and picking one of many possible routes, he spun away between the piles of skeletons that filled this vast hall.

Boy ran and ran, hurtling into pile after pile of bones, making such a terrible noise that he was sure Valerian must be a moment away from catching him.

Finally it was too dark to see at all. Boy staggered on a few more feet, tripped over yet another skull, and collapsed into one of the heaps, too scared of Valerian to worry about what he was lying on.

He lay still, breathing quietly, and realised there was no sound of pursuit. There was no light anywhere. Valerian was probably out in the bone-field somewhere, but Boy seemed to have lost him for now. Without light he could move no further, but Boy was too upset and tired to care. He had passed over and by countless human remains in the last few days. Thousands of bones that were once people, maybe hundreds of thousands, and all because of one man's struggle to avoid joining them.

Boy lay in the bone-field, where the exhumed remains from over-flowing cemeteries all around the City had been moved hundreds of years before to make space for new arrivals. Exhausted, he put his head on to his outstretched arm and amazingly, sleep came for him and took him away.

He woke screaming. He clamped his hand to his mouth and sobbed violently until he felt the panic subsiding. He got to his feet in the darkness and began to walk.

He tried to pretend that he was not blind, that he could see where he was going, and determined to walk until he hit something. He very soon did. It was a wall, but it felt peculiar. He ran his fingers across its surface and felt small strange knobs, each about the size of his fist. He followed the wall and found a corner. Putting his hand out to the right, he found another wall close by that felt the same as the first. He was in another corridor. He put a hand on either wall and began to walk down the corridor as fast as he dared.

The knobs felt funny – smooth and cold, dry despite the general clammy nature of the catacombs. They were evenly spaced, with small gaps between, in an incredibly neat row from the floor to above his head. The whole wall was made of these things stacked in orderly fashion on top of each other. Just as he was trying to work out what they were, his left hand ran over something else in the wall, and he knew what it was instantly.

A skull. It was set into the wall, which Boy realised was made of bones – thigh bones, stacked on top of each other so the thick knobs at the end overlapped and formed the wall.

The panic welled up inside him again and he ran, blind and shrieking, to nowhere.

He ran out through the end of the passageway. Had there been light to see by, and had he stopped to look, he might have seen another inscription above the doorway from which he had emerged.

Stop! This is the Empire of Death.

At least he was going the right way.

6

Valerian prowled on. He had long ago lost Boy.

His arm hurt so much that his mind was clouded by the pain, and yet he could not stop. He knew that his last day must have dawned, but down in this infernal darkness he had no idea what time it was or how long he had left.

The thought made him shudder, and he wondered what was happening in the City, above this subterranean empire. It was presumably going about its normal business, whether sleeping, or waking, or working, or getting ready for the New Year's Eve festival.

The end of the Dead Days, and the end of Valerian's quest, one way or another.

He had to find Boy and he had to find him fast. That was all he knew. Very soon the gates of horror would open and a force would come to hunt over the Earth until he was found, speared and delivered to hell.

Valerian staggered slowly on, his mind fixed on one thing and one thing alone. Boy.

And then, from his right, he felt a breeze on his face. Its freshness was so distinct against the foetid air of the catacombs that he noticed it immediately, and it gave him hope.

Valerian changed course and headed for the breeze. Quickly he came upon another, larger space, where one of the canals passed by, although here for some reason the water flowed as in a fast river. He looked about, saw a doorway, and then a shaft of light rising straight up above his head, and he began to wonder.

Very soon, he began to smile.

He turned back in to the low room, and waited.

7

Kepler led the way, holding the candle in front of him.
Willow clasped the book against her chest. It was so large
and heavy that occasionally they would have to stop while
she shifted it to her other arm. She wanted nothing to do
with the book at all, but Kepler insisted they bring it with
them.

'Can't we leave it here?' she said. 'You were going to hide
it. Can't we do that and come back for it when we've got a
light?'

'Absolutely not!' Kepler said. 'I made that mistake once.
Valerian knows it's down here now. I shall hold on to it – or
rather you will, until we get out.'

So they had made their way across that open square
where Willow, Valerian and Boy had first stepped ashore
after docking their boat behind Kepler's.

'If the other boat's still there, then maybe we have a
chance,' Kepler said.

There was a noise – a cry, and footsteps, coming at them
from the side.

Boy stood in front of them.

'Willow!' he cried, and embraced her. The horrors he had
felt drained away and were replaced by hope, as he held
Willow tight and felt her clasp his hands to her.

'Boy!' she cried, delighted. 'Boy! Boy!'

Swinging her around, Boy saw Kepler too.

'You!' he said.

Boy did not know what to say, because he did not know what he felt.

'You shouldn't have done that,' was all he could blurt out.

'We would have come back for her,' Kepler replied. 'Willow will tell you herself.'

But Willow said nothing.

'We had to get you away from him,' Kepler tried to explain. 'You're the one who's in danger.'

'Why?' cried Boy. 'What does he want me for?'

'Later. All the time you are down here, with Valerian somewhere around, you are in danger. Let us leave this place. It does not lift my spirits, for it provides shelter from everything except death. When we are back in the air of the City I will tell you.'

'The other boat, Boy,' said Willow. 'Hurry.'

There indeed was the boat, still with its pole.

They climbed aboard and with Kepler in front, Willow sitting in the middle clutching the book and Boy holding the pole in the rear, they set off for the outside world.

Many thoughts passed through Boy's mind, but there was one question above all.

'Why does he want to hurt me?' he asked.

Silence.

'One of you answer me!' shouted Boy. 'Answer me! What does he want me for?'

'Don't!' whispered Willow. 'Someone might hear you!'

'So answer me!' shouted Boy.

'He wants your life,' Kepler said coldly. 'Your life is the only way out for him now.'

Boy shook his head in the darkness.

'No,' he said, choking. 'He can't be trying – I don't believe it!'

'Then tell me, Boy, why were you running?' Kepler asked.

Boy said nothing and they drifted on with the current. Kepler started to mutter to himself, then spoke.

'There's a tunnel we must take!' he called. 'On the right, somewhere soon . . . There it is!'

Boy shoved the pole as hard as he could into the bottom of the canal, but the current was strong. He wrestled with the boat and forced it to make the turn, but the pole suddenly held fast in the mud of the canal bottom.

'Quick!' he called. 'Help me!'

The current pulled the boat on. On the point of being pulled in, Boy let the pole go and the boat slipped away. They were now rudderless.

'It doesn't matter,' called Kepler. 'We just need to get to the side up ahead. That's where we get out!'

The canal narrowed even more and the current turned into a powerful surge.

A few more yards and the canal plunged into a small tunnel, across which lay an ancient grille with gaps no wider than a man's hand. The water hurtled through the grille at high speed, off into even more remote depths. The boat smashed into the grille, tearing a gaping hole in its prow.

Willow nearly fell as the boat was pounded again and again against the grille by the relentless force of the water. At least they were going nowhere for the moment. Then, with horror, Boy saw that the grinding of the boat against the decrepit iron grille was starting to weaken it. If it gave way there would be no stopping them from plunging into an even blacker abyss.

Boy had always been led to believe that hell was a hot and fiery place, but he had changed his mind. If hell existed it was this place, here and now. Cold, and wet, and very, very dark.

They clutched at the bank, and with a struggle Willow scrambled on to the stone quayside, throwing the book ahead of her.

She rolled over on to her back and found herself staring up into Valerian's eyes.

'Help them out,' he said to her.

She lay, frozen with terror.

'Help them out!' Valerian screamed at her, and Willow had no choice. In a few more seconds the weight of the boat would have smashed the grille away and they would be lost for ever.

She stretched her arms and pulled Kepler out, then they both did the same for Boy.

They stood facing Valerian.

The book lay between them on the stone flags.

Valerian held Kepler's light device. It began to weaken, and without taking his eyes off it, Valerian put it on the floor and, once again steadying it with his foot, wound the handle until it shone brightly.

He didn't pick it up again.

'So, Boy,' said Valerian.

'Leave him, Valerian,' said Kepler.

'Silence! You traitor! You were supposed to be my friend!'

'I was once. I was. *You* taught *me* about betrayal long ago. Things are not what they once were. You have to admit defeat. You can't take Boy where you should go instead. It's your doing, not his.'

'But now we know what Boy can do for me,' Valerian said, smiling unpleasantly. 'And in this case, I think it's only fitting that he should go instead of me.'

'No!' cried Willow. 'No! You're evil!'

Valerian laughed at her.

'I am not dead! That's all that matters. Now, Boy, come to me!'

Boy began to back away.

Willow and Kepler closed together in front of Boy, trying to keep Valerian from him, but he just laughed.

With his left hand he pulled a slim black tube from inside his coat. He shook it with a flick of his wrist and a spike, long and sharp, hissed out and locked in place with a click. He pointed it at them.

'All I want is the boy,' he said, coming forward again.

They began to circle, Valerian leading the dance, edging them backwards, closer to the canal.

There were three of them against Valerian, with only one good arm but a pointed knife. They stood near the canal bank, Valerian looking beaten, wounded and old. Seeing him like this, their confidence grew and they approached, united in a common purpose.

Boy felt his heart stirring for his master. His end would come now, one way or another. He watched as in slow motion Valerian stuck his stiletto between his teeth, then reached inside his huge black coat one more time.

'No! Stop him!' Boy began, but it was too late.

Valerian's hand flourished back out from the coat in a way that Boy had seen before.

There was a brilliant flash of light which illuminated the whole underground room, and a moment later the space was filled with purple smoke.

'Ho!'

The voice was dry and full of bitter humour – a voice that Boy knew was only Valerian's.

'Ho! And away to Fairyland!'

They choked on the smoke, could still see the flash of

light even with their eyes closed. The smoke took its time to clear, with little air to blow it away, but eventually it began to dissipate.

At last Willow, who had staggered into Kepler, looked around wildly. There was the lamp device Kepler had made lying on the floor, its glow still strong. But that was all.

'He's gone!'

'Valerian!' coughed Kepler, still trying to clear the smoke from his lungs and eyes.

'Oh no!' cried Willow. 'Oh please, no! He's got Boy. He's taken Boy with him!'

'Quick!' Kepler shouted. 'We must save Boy!'

'But how?' she cried. 'He's vanished with his magic again. We can't follow him.'

'Magic?' Kepler said. 'Magic? Valerian has no such thing as magic these days!'

'But I've seen him vanish! And you saw what he just did!'

'No, we did not see what he did! That is only a trick. He must have discovered a way out. An exit to this tombland. A door.

'Look around, Willow! Look around!'

8

Boy felt himself dragged along by the scruff of his neck. A familiar feeling, and he knew it was Valerian doing the pulling. He shuffled along behind him, choking in the smoke, wondering how he had let himself fall for this trick when he had seen it before. He was dragged up a long twisting flight of steps and lost his footing many times, but Valerian seemed to have regained his incredible strength, and Boy felt as if he practically flew up the stairway.

He knew Valerian had no real magic any more. Those days were past – he was just a theatrical showman. But there was a legacy from his dabblings with real magic that awaited them, that was in fact running to meet them with every passing second.

As the smoke cleared from Boy's eyes, and they stopped watering, he began to look around, and what he saw shocked him more than anything.

They were outside.

Not only that, but they were outside in the garden of the Yellow House.

'How – how did we get here?' coughed Boy.

'Simple enough', said Valerian, 'when you work out where

you are. I knew a little, I guessed the rest. Took me longer than it should have. Now be quiet and do as you're told.'

Boy felt the past tickle his mind, and he remembered days when he had sat in the garden and dreamt he could hear running water. It seemed he had not dreamt it after all.

He turned to break away but froze as he felt the point of Valerian's knife at his neck.

'One more inch,' he hissed. 'One more inch and it's your last. Now get up the stairs.'

Valerian, fumbling with keys while holding the knife, shoved open the back door to the Yellow House, which led into the kitchens. He pushed Boy ahead of him.

'Hurry! There's little time!'

They made their way into the halls as the clocks chimed a quarter to the hour.

But which hour?

'Damnation!' cried Valerian. 'Midnight!'

He urged Boy up the stairs, up, up, up, all the way to the Tower.

Valerian kicked the door open, thrust Boy through, and slammed it shut behind him.

Locking the door, he put the key in his pocket and staggered over to the camera obscura. He began to adjust its controls, swearing loudly when he was clumsy with his only usable hand.

'Valerian,' Boy said, but his master held up his hand.

'Shut your mouth, Boy!' Valerian screamed, whirling round to face him. 'Shut. Your. Mouth. Say nothing. Do nothing.'

'But–'

'I said, be quiet!'

Boy said nothing. Valerian closed his eyes for a moment or two, then fiddled with the focus of the camera again. Satisfied, he began to scan the streets around the House. Boy heard him speaking softly to himself.

> 'The stars still move, time still runs,
> the clocks will strike, the devil will come.'

After a while, finding nothing unusual, he gave it up.

'Perhaps Kepler was right,' Valerian said, turning back to Boy. 'Maybe it was a waste of money, but I'm not beaten yet.'

He moved over to sit in his armchair.

'Now all we have to do is wait. In a few minutes, it will come. The time will come. Then you go instead of me, and I am saved. I hope that's clear.'

It seemed to Boy as if Valerian was asking him a question.

'No,' he said.

'Be quiet!' Valerian shouted. 'It is not for you to ask. You have served me all these years; you are going to do this last thing for me.'

Outside, it was snowing heavily. There was a sudden bang and flash of light outside the window. Valerian jumped from his seat and hurried to the camera's projection.

Then they both saw the twinkle of fireworks scatter across the City sky, and Valerian slunk back to his chair. They heard the sounds of revellers from the New Year's Eve parties winding through the street below.

'People having fun,' he said. 'Something to celebrate. Well, I shall have something to celebrate too, very soon.'

He glanced at one of his clocks on the wall of the Tower room. Boy looked about desperately. The camera obscura, the tricks, the stage props, the experiments, the chemicals. He could see no help from anything.

'How can you do this to me? I've done nothing to hurt you. I've helped you all I can, but I don't want–'

'To die? No, neither do I, Boy. That's why you're going to instead of me.'

'But I don't understand!' shouted Boy. 'Why me, of all people?'

'That is something of a joke. It is precisely you, of all people, and only you, that can save me. We were meant to be together, you and I. When you fell from the ceiling in the church, that was meant to be, too.'

Boy stood staring at his master. He had mistreated him, beaten him, shouted at him. That much was true, but he had also helped him, fed him and clothed him, after a fashion. He couldn't believe that Valerian was really going to send him to his death.

'But why? Why me?'

'You are the solution,' said Valerian evenly. 'That is what the book told me. There you were, right in front of me all the time. I know this now, as Kepler does. *You* are the answer.'

Boy shook his head dumbly.

The clock on the wall ticked on and its long hand slid another minute closer to midnight.

'Fifteen years ago – fifteen years ago I made a bargain. I told you that. With a terrible price to pay at the end. What I didn't tell you is what I couldn't know. When I made the pact, something else was created then, too. *Someone*, I should say. Another soul.'

Boy shook his head again, not wanting to believe what he was hearing. The clock clunked and whirred. One minute to midnight.

'What . . .' he stammered, 'What?'

'Not what, Boy, but who. You. You were conceived on the very evening that I made my bargain, fifteen years ago on New Year's Eve. You are a vessel for me to use. This was what the book told me, and it also told me, as it must have

258

told Kepler, about the only way out. A life the same age, as measured from conception, as the term of the pact. So you go instead of me. Then the bargain will be satisfied and I shall walk free.'

'But I'll die!'

'Yes,' said Valerian, 'but I won't.'

The clock, precise instrument that it was, began to sound midnight. As its twelve chimes died, the thing began to come.

The room was filled with light, and this time they knew it was no firework. The light was as bright as day, brighter even, and behind it came a great wind which lifted up all the loose papers in the room and swirled them madly around.

Boy staggered backwards and fell to the floor. Valerian rose to his feet, struggling against the storm that had entered the room, the tails of his great black coat waving in the vortex of wind.

Boy peered up at the light, which had now developed a black hole in its centre. Small at first, the black hole grew in size until there was a swirling darkness the size and shape of a man hovering just above the floor.

Then came a voice. At least, Boy thought it was a voice, but there was no one to say the words. He simply heard the words in his head and all around him. The voice was small and quiet, but strangely could be clearly heard. It was flat and colourless.

'Valerian, your time has come. Step forward.'

Boy felt a surge of pain, a mental pain that left him rigid with fear.

Valerian stood, swaying slightly in front of the hole.

'No,' he said, his voice wavering, 'No. The boy will go instead of me.'

There was silence.

'Is that not my right?' asked Valerian.

259

'Send the boy forward.'

And Valerian turned to Boy.

'Get up,' he said coldly.

Boy didn't move.

'Get up!'

This time he roared the words, and Boy automatically got to his feet. It was *what he did*, he thought. *What he did* was do what Valerian told him.

'Am I really just an empty vessel?' he asked Valerian quietly.

Valerian nodded.

'You are just a vessel, and you have served your purpose. You were made for me. I am your only family, and your family needs you.'

'No!' cried Boy. 'You're not my family. I must have a mother and father! Everyone does.'

'Not you, Boy. You don't even have a name.'

'You could have given me one. Why didn't you?'

Behind them the blackness swirled angrily, evil colours pouring from within it.

The voice came again.

'It is time! Step forward!'

'You could have given me a name if you'd ever cared about me!' cried Boy. 'But you never did! All you ever did was hurt me and shout at me and tell me I'm stupid, and kick me and threaten me! I've spent my life running around the City, in dark holes, in dangerous places, and you never cared! Not ever!'

'Boy–' said Valerian.

'Don't call me that! I want a real name! I want to know who I am, not this nonsense! I must have a life. I must have. This can't be *all* I am!'

Valerian looked at Boy. He seemed to be about to speak

but said nothing, and turned to look at the rushing nothing-ness which threatened to engulf the whole room.

And then there was another sound. It was a thump at the Tower door. Valerian did not hear it. His whole attention was fixed on the inky centre of the vortex.

The thump came again, and once more, and Kepler and Willow burst into the room, the door flying wide on its ancient hinges, bits of wood from the splintered lock scatter-ing across the floor. In a glance they saw the horror in the room.

'No!' screamed Kepler. 'No!'

Valerian turned to face him.

'You!' he threw back. 'You! What right have you to tell me to do anything?'

'Valerian! No, no, no! You must not kill Boy! You must not.'

Willow ran to Boy and they clung to each other, cowering in the maelstrom that filled the room. Unheard, other, less precise clocks all around the house chimed midnight.

'You cannot kill him,' Kepler repeated.

'And why not?' sneered Valerian. 'Tell me why not! He is mine, he has always been mine, and I will do with him as I like!'

'Yes, he is yours,' Kepler pleaded, desperation tearing his expression into a sickening gape.

'He is my slave, and—'

'No, Valerian! No! He is your son,' and Kepler took a step towards Valerian.

'Don't be—'

'I said, he is your son!' Kepler shouted, raising a fist to-wards Valerian.

Valerian stopped, as if physically struck. He said nothing. He seemed to be thinking.

261

'I saw it in the book! It is the truth. Think about his age, Valerian. His age!'

Boy stood, struggling to get to his feet. He turned to Valerian.

Valerian stared deep into his eyes. He felt Valerian coming for him, as so often before, through his eyes, feeling for his soul, but this time it was different. He was not controlling, not manipulating, but feeling, sensing.

Boy felt his master's mind walk through his, as if for the first time really seeing what was there, finally understanding Boy's life. The years on his own, living off his wits on the harsh City streets. Being found by Valerian, hoping for so much but getting so little.

Valerian found that his own pain was nothing compared with Boy's.

He pulled away and stepped back, but still he looked deep into Boy's eyes.

He stepped backwards towards the swirling pit, and backwards once more, and fell into the darkness, already a dead man.

He spoke one more word as he went.

'Boy!'

Boy stood, numb.

The hole, the light, the wind disappeared faster than they had come, and Boy stared into space. All that remained was a faint wisp of yellow smoke that hung in the air, and a pungent smell that vexed their nostrils.

Valerian was gone.

Willow rushed to Boy and held him in her arms while he screamed and screamed.

Eventually his screams subsided and became cries and then the cries became tears, and he sat, staring at Willow.

'He went. He changed his mind. He let me live.'

'Don't talk,' said Willow. 'Not now.'

'But there's so much I don't understand. My father . . . my father?'

He turned to Kepler who stood looking down at him, a strange expression on his face.

'Was he – was he really my father?' Boy said.

Kepler looked hard at Boy. Long seconds passed, in which he said nothing.

'Was he my father? Tell me!' Boy said, more urgently this time.

'Of course he wasn't,' Kepler snapped. 'Don't be ridiculous. I just said that to make you live. I knew it was the only thing I could say that might save you.'

'No!' cried Boy, 'No! You're lying. You're lying now! You said I was his son.'

'There are things you don't know about, Boy,' said Kepler. 'Things that happened long ago. I was simply using those things to save your life.'

He turned to the door.

'No!' cried Boy, 'Wait . . .'

'You're alive, aren't you, Boy? Just be grateful for that.'

Kepler stooped, and picked up the book from the floor where Willow had dropped it.

'I'll see you're all right,' said Kepler. 'Both of you. Now that Valerian's gone.'

He walked out through the shattered doorway.

Boy collapsed into Willow's arms, and began to sob once more. Around them lay the devastation of what had once been the heart of Valerian's world. From the streets below came the noise of happy, drunken people, and from the skies overhead came the rush and bang of fireworks.

A long time passed. Boy's tears flowed freely down his face, Willow holding him all the while. He thought about what he'd heard, what he'd seen, but couldn't begin to understand. He pushed the thoughts away.

There would be time enough to think, later.

And there was something else. Someone else.

As if only now noticing her, Boy felt Willow's arms around him. He lifted his head, and looked up at her face, and at last he saw the love that was waiting for him there.

A new year had dawned, with a new, and different future, one that Boy had not foreseen. He sensed that the path ahead was obscured by many, many questions, but one thing, at least, was clear.

Boy and Willow would walk that path together.

from
The Dark Flight Down
the sequel to
The Book of Dead Days

prologue

Midnight at the Imperial Court of Emperor Frederick III. The court has been emptied for the evening of its usual crowd of sycophants and entertainers, of its alchemists, astrologers, doctors, faith-healers, druggists, noblemen, ne'er-do-wells, priests, actors and occultists.

The Emperor sits on his throne, apparently alone, brooding. He lifts a pale hand, slowly, lazily.

'Maxim!' he calls, in his high, pathetic voice. 'Dammit, Maxim, where are you?'

From the shadows behind the throne a tall, heavy figure emerges, swathed in a dark red robe that trails in the dust on the marble Court floor. Maxim, the Emperor's right-hand, his confidant and oracle.

'Sire?' Maxim says. He is tired, but careful to show no sign of this to Frederick. He runs a hand across the top of his shaven head.

'There you are!' Frederick declares, but without emotion. 'There you are.'

'Sire,' Maxim says, ready to do the Emperor's bidding.

'Maxim, how many years have I left to live?'

Maxim hesitates briefly before answering, wondering how many times he has had this conversation with the Emperor, and then, more depressingly, he wonders how many *more* times he will have it.

267

'Sire, we have established beyond all possible doubt that you will live to a venerable age.'

He bows, to try to emphasise the significance of his words, hoping they will be sufficient to keep Frederick happy.

'Yes, yes,' says Frederick, far from happy. He lifts a long thin finger and scratches the side of his nose. Flakes of skin float into the gloom of the deserted Court. 'But how long exactly, would you say?'

Maxim sighs inwardly. It is not to be short, then.

'Ah!' he says brightly. 'Well, our finest thinkers are convinced that you will live to be . . . a hundred!'

Frederick is silent for a while. Maxim begins to back away.

'But what then?' Frederick cries suddenly.

Maxim hurries back to the foot of the throne.

'Well,' he says. 'Well! We have every right, every reason, to suppose that you will live to be a hundred and twenty. There is no reason why not.'

'Ah. I see. One hundred. And twenty.'

'Sire,' says Maxim, wondering if he dare retire from the Emperor's presence.

'But! But what then? What then, Maxim? What. Then.'

Maxim is tired, and would very much like to be upstairs in his chambers, asleep, but he knows there is little chance of that now. Still, he is careful to show no sign of his tiredness, his irritation.

'Sire, your Excellency may then have the good grace to die.'

That should shut him up, Maxim thinks, bowing his large frame as low as he can manage without falling onto his nose.

'Die?' Frederick whines. 'Die? And what then?'

Maxim jerks his head upright, now irritated beyond reason by the Emperor's voice.

'Well, Sire,' he says slowly, gazing at the ceiling, 'there'll be . . . mourning. A period of great sorrow across the whole City. People will . . . stop to remember the great Frederick, and celebrate. They'll make . . .'

Maxim hesitates, inspiration deserting him. He looks down, and finds the Emperor scowling at him.

'They'll make . . . ?'

'Yes, Sire,' says Maxim. 'They'll make . . . boom boom.'

'Boom boom?' Frederick asks. 'They'll make boom boom? What in heaven's name do you mean? A celebration? Fireworks? Is that it? Is that all I will have to show for my time?'

Maxim lifts his head to the Emperor, opens his hands wide, and for once, is at a loss for words.

Frederick rises to his feet. Even standing, his short, skinny frame is dwarfed by his towering throne.

He points at Maxim.

'They will not make 'boom boom' because I am not going to die! Not ever. I will reach one hundred, and then another one after that, and then another after that. Do you see, Maxim? Do you? I am the last of the line, Maxim, you know that as well as anyone. I have no kith, Maxim, no kin, no offspring, nor progeny. If I die, the chain is broken. The end is reached. The Empire will have no Emperor. There is only one answer. I am not going to die! You, my loyal servant, will see to it. I am not to die, and you are going to make sure of it.'

Maxim hesitated. The Emperor was a fool. And he was a liar too. Some things could not be forgotten, could not be hidden as easily as Frederick would have liked, but Maxim wasn't going to tell him that.

'But, Sire, I . . .'

'No, it is no use. I have made up my mind. Either you find a way to make me immortal, or your own end will be swifter than you might expect. Now get out of my sight, and find someone to carry me up to bed. You have no idea how bad it is for me, sitting on this throne all day.'

'No, Sire,' says Maxim, his hand already pulling a bell-rope.

'And don't forget! Find a way to make me live for ever. Or . . .'

And Maxim watches with a familiar prickle of horror as the feeble old Emperor whisks a skinny finger across his own throat.

'Phht!'

Boy is about to come face to face with Frederick and Maxim, plunged into the heart of their desperate scheming and cruel tricks. Here, amidst the golden, crumbling splendour of the Royal Court, his very life will come to depend upon the whim of madmen, as he struggles to escape the half-forgotten horror waiting for him at the foot of the Dark Flight Down.

Also by Marcus Sedgwick

The Dark Horse

A girl snatched from the wolves, a sealed box that can only be opened by one person, a sinister stranger with black-palmed hands nearing the end of his quest, and a boy destined to lead his clan are woven together in this riveting story of betrayal and ancient magic.

Set in a distant time, in a distant place, the Storn live quietly, fishing and farming, eking out what living they can. But on the day of the wolf hunt their lives will change forever. That's the day Sig rescues a small, ragged, howling child, more like the wolves she came from than a human being. They call her Mouse, but who is she really? What is her secret? Years later, they find out. The shocking discovery of her true identity brings to life a terrifying legend and plunges them all into treachery and a cruelty from which there is no escape.

Mystery, intrigue and danger blaze through the darkness of Marcus Sedgwick's extraordinary third novel.

Shortlisted for the Carnegie Medal and the Guardian Children's Fiction Award.

'. . . a highly charged, timeless mystery . . . Sparely told, rich in imagination'   *Guardian*

'never ceases to be gripping.'   *Sunday Telegraph*

'an intriguing read . . . This world, so different from our own, is very well chronicled and convincing . . . Totally unexpected and terrifying, but completely believable.'   *Carousel*

'carefully crafted'   *Irish Times*

'the saga is strange, enigmatic and wholly original.'   *Daily Telegraph*

'An engrossing story with a mythical quality . . .'   *Time Out*

'The plot is pacy and fast moving with plenty of action.'
                                                    School Librarian

Floodland

Imagine that England is covered by water, and Norwich is an island . . .

Zoe, left behind in the confusion when her parents escaped, survives there as best she can. Alone and desperate among marauding gangs, she manages to dig a derelict boat out of the mud and gets away to Eels Island. But Eels Island, whose raggle-taggle inhabitants are dominated by the strange boy Dooby, is full of danger too.

The belief that she will one day find her parents spurs Zoe on to a dramatic escape in a wonderful story of courage and determination, set in the watery landscape of England as it could be a few years from now.

Winner of the Branford Boase Award.

Witch Hill

The fire was a family tragedy that Jamie can't forget. Fire dominates his waking thoughts and haunts his dreams.

And there is something else going on in the village of Crownhill. Something terrifying to do with an evil old witch who gets into his dreams, determined to do him harm, and a scared girl, the victim of a witch hunt. Jamie senses her presence all around. If only he could cross the barriers of time and save her . . .

A present-day boy, a seventeenth-century girl, an ancient crone: for a single moment in time, their lives are fused by fire. And as the dark secrets of Crownhill and its witches are revealed, Jamie has to confront his worst fears in order to free himself from the horrors of the past.

An extraordinary and compelling novel from Marcus Sedgwick, whose first book, *Floodland*, was hailed as 'a dazzling debut'.

'a skilfully knitted piece of storytelling.' *Independent on Saturday*

'a gripping intelligent read.' *Telegraph*

'a very readable psychological thriller, in which clever twists maintain the tension throughout.' *Books for Keeps*